To P. +

D1706776

The Gentlemen's Rooming House

Stephanie Sunshine Pincus

Enjoy!) Lots of Love

Stephanie Sunshine

XXOO

CreateSpace
North Charleston, South Carolina USA

CreateSpace
North Charleston, South Carolina USA

ISBN-13: 978-1515161196

ISBN-10: 1515161196

Current Printing: 1

Printed in the United States of America

Library of Congress Control Number: 2015909572

Thank You

To my wonderful husband Richard, who typed each and every chapter, and lovingly did so.

To my creative daughter Angela who besides my illustrations, did a fabulous job of print work and color coordination of the front and back cover.

579-6229

Biography

Stephanie Sunshine Pincus is a true renaissance woman. She has lived life fully with all of her talents, smarts and creativity. She has been a gerontologist helping the elderly, has exhibited her art work all over the country, has been a teacher, mentor and life coach. This is her second book published, but her first novel. She lives in Tucson, Arizona with her husband and son.

PS

Many of the heroine's issues in the novel including her fibromyalgia come from Stephanie's real life.

List of Characters

1. Lucy (heroine)

2. Mom and Dad

3. Adam (Lucy's brother who died)

4. Jake (former fiancé who died)

5. The Cats – (Lando, Yoda, and Callie)

6. Agnes (The nurse – housekeeper)

7. Paul and Joe (roomers)

8. Isaac (roomer)

9. Andy (roomer)

10. Marty (roomer)

11. Claire (Lucy's friend and Marty's girlfriend)

12. Omar (roomer)

13. James and Roger (fellow roomer)

14. Ezra and Leon (father and son fellow roomers)

15. Esteban (Lucy's fiancé)

16. David (Lucy's old love)

17. Jaime and Roberta (Esteban's parents)

18. Irisa and Ralph (the children)

19. Rabbi Thomas Louchheim

Table of Contents

Chapter 1

About the Book

The Gentlemen's Rooming House is a beautiful simple story of a strong, exciting but vulnerable woman owning a rooming house for gentlemen only.

The characters and storyline came to me one night while I was sleeping; and when I woke up everything came back to me like I lived the experience myself. I was there! I met all the characters and through the entire writing experience, they became my family and my friends. I got to love each one of them. The characters are real, living their lives everyday with their problems, joys and love affairs.

The book has some sex in it, but no whips and chains – just plain old sex!

When you read this book, you will discover that the author's life takes place in every character, and especially Lucy.

The book is warm and fuzzy, but also a bit mysterious, exciting and sensual.

Enjoy, Enjoy!

1

The Gentlemen's Rooming House

Chapter 2

Rio Rico (Rich River)

The Big House stood in the middle of Rio Rico land, not far from the big and famous hotel and golf resort. Rio Rico is a southeastern Arizona community of approximately 18,000 residents. It has an elevation of about 3,500 feet, and the sun shines almost every day.

Rio Rico is in an area where Spanish and Indian families lived generations before the American Revolution, and where Arizona history began. Rio Rico covers 39,000 acres in Santa Cruz county, 10 miles north of the US-Mexico international border and about 55 miles south of Tucson.

The area is magnificent with lots of small wildlife, lots of vegetation, a great number of various species of birds, and a number of famous golf courses. A great number of vegetative crops feed the town and are shipped all over Arizona.

The Gentlemen's Rooming House

Chapter 3

The Property

The property was almost four acres large. It was mainly covered with trees – large and small – but mainly weeping willows. There were bushes of all kinds and sizes – especially flowering bushes in the summer. There was also some grass, lots of sandy, stony areas, leaves and pine cones that covered the ground. When the moon shone at night over the willow trees, the property looked very eerie, and even scary! There was a rumor that at one time bats used to fly around the property.

It was a four story building with two verandas, a large patio to the right, and a very big separate garage building to the left. There was also a great indoor porch in the front of the house, bringing in wonderful sunshine almost all day long. Mom and Lucy fell in love with the property when they first saw it in Rio Rico, when riding through the area years before. It had such charm and character that the women believed it could become a winning investment for the future.

Mom spent almost eight hundred thousand dollars for the property and over one quarter million dollars to reconstruct, refurbish and beautify it. They found very reasonable contractors and workmen to fix up the building and the grounds.

When the building was finished it looked exquisite and very regal. The building was painted beige, white and black, including the roof. The kitchen and bathrooms were redone The fixtures and some of the appliances were replaced, along with the windows and some of the plumbing. The structure of the house was excellent.

Mom and Lucy loved the nineteenth century old world charm of the house and believed it held many interesting stories and secrets behind its walls. The property was empty for many years Now it was time to give the house a new life.

Chapter 4

The Big House

There were ten bedroom units in the house and a full two bedroom unit in the new large refurbished garage. This unit had a full bath and kitchenette. There was also a good-size storage center for supplies in the garage too – but completely separate from the two bedroom unit. The other bedroom units were on the second, third and fourth floors. Each two bedrooms had a shared full bathroom and a good-size kitchenette.

On the first floor was the bright inside porch filled with chairs, lounges and small tables. Potted flowering plants were placed everywhere for color and freshness. Lucy always tried to bring nature inside the house. The huge modern kitchen had a table capable of seating more than ten people. There were shiny matching appliances, and a large cupboard. The laundry room had two coin operated washers and dryers for the roomers. Nearby was a large pantry loaded with groceries and a special area for the kitties – where they ate, drank and did their business. There was a very large living room /

7

dining room combination, with two sofas, two comfortable chairs, two tables with lamps, and a table large enough to seat at least twenty people. The room was stunning but still remained cozy. There was also lots of closets and storage spaces for the roomers' bulky belongings, and a large double shed outside. Behind the kitchen there were two large bathrooms and a beautiful sitting room.

On the second floor was Mom's large bedroom suite with a full bath, veranda and outside porch. Also, there was Lucy's large bedroom, a dressing room, a large bathroom and Lucy's library. She loved books – reading them and collecting them. There was also a large walk-in closet and Lucy's office. Nearby was a small laundry room with a washer, dryer and folding table for Mom's, Lucy's and Agnes's clothes, linens and towels.

The extra bedroom unit on the second floor was always saved for David, a forty-five year old military man. He came to Rio Rico four times a year for four to five weeks at a time. He was a military software genius, and he came to work at Davis-Monthan Air Force Base in Tucson. David fell in love with Rio Rico a few years back when he stayed at the big resort there. Rio Rico was only fifty to sixty minutes away from the air force base, and David was willing to make that trip. It was a beautiful ride. He wanted a homey atmosphere when he stayed in Arizona, and heard about Lucy's house about three years ago. He met Lucy, saw the house, the property, and the atmosphere, and it was like at first sight. He loved the home-cooked meals in the big kitchen, and he adored Lucy.

David was short, but very muscular. He was almost stocky in build – but trim. He had an incredible smile with beautiful perfect teeth; Lucy loved perfect white and sparkling teeth. She brushed her teeth four times a day. Lucy also admired his ruggedness. He wasn't handsome, but he was very sensual.

David and Lucy hit it off when they first met, and they romanced each other every time he stayed in Rio Rico.

David was married to Lynn for over thirteen years and they had two boys. His wife was a true runaround wife. She partied all the time when he was home and when he was away. She had a reputation for sleeping with the most attractive men in the area. David just allowed her to do her thing, because he just lived his own life

9

with his boys. They met in college and married two and one-half to three years after graduation. She was extremely beautiful and sexy. Her personality showed off, but her character was questionable as David found out later. He slowly drew away from her. He was somewhat of an introvert – quiet, serious, intellectual. Lynn was none of those things.

David never cheated at home – a little town outside of Madison, Wisconsin. However, when he came to the big house, he and Lucy slept together often. They read poetry together, enjoyed concerts, and loved the arts. Lucy respected David's intellect, his sensitivity and his gentleness. He also bought Lucy trinkets and books, and even bought her a diamond pendant. Lucy cared a lot for David, but always knew he would never leave his wife because of the boys. This was just a part-time love affair – and Lucy needed more.

On the third floor was a two bedroom suite with a full bathroom and kitchenette. This suite was for Paul and Joe – the two brothers. Also, on the other side of the floor was another identical two bedroom suite with a full bathroom and kitchenette. This suite was occupied by James and Roger – the gay partners.

On the fourth floor was a duplicate floor plan of the third floor. Two bedroom suites were located on the left and right sides of the floor. The roomers were Andy and Isaac, and on the right were Omar and Marty.

Chapter 5

The Furnishings

The furnishings inside the house were unique. There was old and new, antique and modern. Things that were bought and collected from all over the country, and even some old classic pieces from Mexico and Spain. There were things bought from several old shops in Mexico, since Rio Rico was a stone's throw from the border. The women got friendly with an old Mexican family in Nogales who owned a small factory. They made the women some fabulous pieces of vintage looking furniture and unique old brass lamps and chandeliers. How wonderful the house was shaping up. Inside the house was light, joy and beauty. Love permeated every inch of the building and it sparkled with cleanliness.

The Gentlemen's Rooming House

Chapter 6

Lucy

Lucy was thirty-nine years old. She was short, five foot one and one-half inches. She was petite, but her body appeared much taller as she always stood up straight. Her hair extremely thick and shiny was very brown-black in color. Her short dark curls surrounded her face like a beautiful bonnet. She thought her hair was her best feature, but Lucy had many other great features. Her alabaster skin was smooth except for a small red birthmark on her upper left cheek. The mark was almost pleasant to look at as it resembled a pretty color of blush on her cheek. However, she had to put actual blush on her right cheek to match the left. Lucy had slanty brown-black eyes and very full eyelashes. She didn't have to wear much mascara. Her eyes appeared dark and sad at times, especially when she was in pain. Her extremely large eyes almost swallowed up her face. Lucy's lips were rather fine and sometimes pouty. Her ears were small and close to her face. Lucy's nose was a perfect Irish pug nose – but she wasn't even Irish.

Lucy had a beautiful figure – her breasts were large, her waist small, and her hips were fully shaped. She had lovely legs however short, with small but outstanding blue veins peeking through. She often wore support stockings, as she was on her feet all day long. Lucy's hands were small but very strong. Her manicured long nails were always painted hot red pink.

Much of Lucy's look came from her dad. He was very Italian, and had very dark Mediterranean looks. He was handsome enough to have been a big movie and screen star.

Lucy was always conscious of her weight as she lost over thirty-five pounds with the Weight Watchers diet system, and she didn't want to gain an ounce back. Most of her life she had been pleasantly plump, and she believed she was big-boned. However, after losing so much weight she found out that she was only medium-boned, petite and svelte. She also learned of her slow metabolism, and had to start taking thyroid medication. Lucy was so proud of her new figure, and loved showing off in clingy curve-fitting, flattering clothes. Lucy did wear appropriate clothes when working in the house.

Lucy had her hair done faithfully every Wednesday morning. Greta was her longtime hairdresser, friend, and confidante. Sometimes she didn't feel good enough to drive herself, but Marty would always offer help with his cab. Lucy was sensitive about asking for help from anyone, but her roomers were her friends. They helped each other. They were all remarkable people.

Lucy was a feisty girl and she needed and craved affection, attention and love-making. Even when she was a little girl she would masturbate herself to sleep. She was always restless. She had a deep, ever present and relentless need for touching, fondling and sexual release. She was sweet and feminine, but she was almost always in control. She knew the ropes and knew how to handle the men. However strong in character, Lucy had a very emotional, and vulnerable side to her. She was a true Gemini. She was a complete paradox of emotions inside that little body. A man once told her that if an alien came to earth and asked for a woman they would take the alien right to Lucy.

Lucy was a smart businesswoman. She handled all the management duties of the house, and also the accounting, purchasing and decorating work. She knew how to keep order in the house, and also how to please the gentleman roomers. She was very good to everyone and everyone loved her. Sometimes she was opinionated and had a big mouth, but she usually was correct in her beliefs. She was always honest to a fault, but she could also admit if she was wrong.

She was a most interesting specimen of femininity, strength of character, dignity and class. She was a little girl and an old soul wrapped in one. She was passionate and compassionate. She was very complicated.

Lucy had many talents also. She loved to dance – oh she loved to dance, with anyone, at anytime – even when she was cooking or cleaning. She loved reading poetry and also writing it. She loved writing and kept a daily journal on her desk. She also loved art, and worked in five different mediums. Mom loved to see her paint – with all her brushes sticking out of her pockets.

Lucy had specific things in her life that she loved, treasured and on which she spent her money. She loved – loved – loved beautiful and exciting clothes. She had three closets filled with conservative suits, beautiful sexy dresses, pants outfits and luxurious sweaters. She also had many lounging outfits for those moments she needed to rest and relax. She had three jewelry boxes plus an armoire filled with bling – gorgeous unique pieces of jewelry that made her happy and brightened her life. She had collected her jewelry since the age of twelve. She often watched the television shopping channels for specials and good buys. The TV helped her relax, especially when she was in pain. Lucy usually wore comfortable shoes while working, however she had stacks of boxes of fabulous sultry shoes of all styles in her closets. She just loved to look at them. She wore them only when she went out, or for special occasions, and only for a few hours at a time.

The Gentlemen's Rooming House

Chapter 7

Mom and Dad

Mom was very ill for a long time. She was frail, weak and was a little lady. Her cancer started many years ago and eventually ran through much of her body. Her cancer was like a slow, but very constant current of flowing toxins, carrying with it enemies of pain and destruction. Mom always worked years ago as a high school teacher, and kids and adults always loved and respected her. She was a real lady in the true sense of the word.

Lucy loved her mom very much, and did whatever she could to make her life easier. Thank G-d Lucy and Mom could afford Agnes as Mom's private nurse.

Mom brought up Lucy with dignity, honor, and the appreciation of life and all it had to offer. She taught her love, devotion and a knack for making good decisions. She also taught her responsibility and a good work ethic. Lucy knew how to save money – and how to make money.

Lucy wanted Mom to remain as comfortable as possible in her final months – even though Mom hardly ever complained. Mom's name was Rachel – and she loved flowers. Lucy had a bunch of potted plants and flowers in the veranda outside Mom's bedroom. Mom loved the colors – and the sunshine glowing on the flowers in bloom.

Mom met Dad (Michael) when she was twenty-four years old and he was twenty-nine. He was a CPA. They met at a concert where they virtually bumped into each other at the snack stand. They apologized, dated, and were married six months later.

Dad was a kind, gentle, and a very generous man. He always was very calm even around tax time. He always knew the right answers, and even helped start a free service for young people who needed their taxes done, but couldn't really afford to pay a fee. They were so grateful to him that they often gave him homemade dishes and pastries on major holidays.

Dad died in an automobile accident eleven and one-half years ago. He was a really good man, but was in the wrong place at the wrong time. He was stopping at a red light when a speeding police car didn't judge its distance when turning the corner where Dad was stopped. The police car, riding almost eighty-five miles an hour, smashed into Dad's car and almost demolished it. Dad was dead on impact, but the other policeman driver lived. Mom, after more than two years of grieving and shock, received a hefty settlement from the police department. It was more than three million dollars. It provided security for Mom and Lucy and it bought them their future – it bought them the rooming house. And, as Mom always said, "Only rent to men, they're less trouble." So, Mom and Lucy bought a big, very old mansion–like property that looked like it belonged in an old movie. And, they opened up the Gentlemen's Rooming House after nearly two years of reconstruction and refurbishing.

The Gentlemen's Rooming House

Chapter 8

Adam

Lucy had a brother Adam who was killed at the end of the Vietnam war. He was only nineteen years old. He was the first born of the children, and the first to die. He was short but muscular, and he had black curly hair like Lucy. His eyes were piercing blue like Dad's eyes – and he looked straight in the eyes when he looked at you. Lucy didn't know him very well as there was a big age difference between them, and, he left to enlist in the Army so young. Lucy remembered his strong personality, his smarts and his courage. He only insisted that he wanted to help his country, and to do his part. Mama and Lucy talked about him often, and remembered him with love and devotion.

The Gentlemen's Rooming House

Chapter 9

Jake

Lucy was never married, but got very close many years ago. She even had her wedding dress ordered, and the invitations sent out in the mail. She remembered how excited she was, how the memories were still fresh in her mind. Mom had purchased a very expensive and luxurious hope chest for her – filled with silks and ribbons and lace. Lucy was going to be a magnificent bride. But what a disastrous ending that dream became. Two weeks, four days and six hours before the wedding was to take place in a large hotel in Tucson, Jake – that was his wonderful name – had an acute heart attack at the age of twenty-nine. It was found out later that Jake had very high blood pressure, and never realized it or was treated for it.

Lucy was twenty-five years old at the time, and now, fourteen years later, she still suffered from shattered dreams syndrome. That's what she called it. Since than, Lucy had dated some nice and different men, but none fit the bill, like Jake did. She loved and respected Jake so much. He had been like her idol.

27

Lucy spent six months in therapy, and three weeks in the psychiatric ward of a private nearby sanatorium for extreme anxiety, depression and the beginning of fibromyalgia pain. Indeed it was the onset of her fibro syndrome.

Chapter 10

The Cats

Lucy's almost favorite things in the whole world besides her mom, the men, and the big house were her pet cats. She had three of them and they loved her as well. Especially when Lucy stepped into the pantry to fetch their food, and especially their treats, they stood in line, one by one at attention. The three cats were Lando, Callie and Yoda. Yoda was the baby – he could be the instigator and the fighter, but he always was the charmer. He was a very handsome black and white house cat with big beautiful eyes and a very pink nose. Lando was the oldest male – very reserved, manly, quiet and a real gentleman cat. He was a true tabby – black, gray and white.

He didn't want trouble and didn't look for it. He was abused when he was little with former owners, and he got frightened a lot with loud or abrupt noises or movements. They were all big cats but Yoda and Callie were just plain fat or plump. The kitties loved Lucy and rubbed against her and ran around her all the time. Lando and Yoda got along but Yoda stalked Callie until she screamed.

29

Let's talk about Callie the calico cat – beautiful orange, white, and black. They all called her the Halloween girlie. She was long-haired and had knots all over. She was obsessed with being clean, and washed herself day and night. She licked so much, she had twisted hair all over. Lucy had to cut out many knotted patches of fur, especially around her butt. Lucy brushed her the most and she loved it. She would roll around and roll over. Callie was also called the girlie because she walked swaying her hips and shook her tush. She acted like a diva. Callie also had a little black mustache near her lips, and she often looked like Charlie Chaplin. Callie knew when Lucy hurt a lot, and she often slept next to her in bed to comfort her. Lucy owned Callie the longest, and they both truly understood each other. Yoda would run after Callie all day long – he wanted to play with her, but the girlie wanted nothing to do with him. She would have to run into the pantry under the big table to hide from him. She would hiss and hide, and Yoda would try to hit and sock her. Sometimes Callie punched back. The kitties were a full time job, but all the roomers loved them too.

Chapter 11

Agnes

Mom's nurse Agnes was an elderly woman, almost as old as mom who was seventy-two years old, and Agnes was seventy. At two hundred and seventy-five pounds and at five foot three inches tall, she was a pretty large presence in the house compared to Mom's very thin, fragile, and slight build. Agnes was also an African-American lady. Agnes came to take care of Mom every day for four to five hours, except for Sundays. She bathed, dressed, and gave her all of her medications, except for Mom's nighttime sleeping pills which Lucy gave her.

Agnes was very professional, and she and Mom really were close and loved each other. They were pals! Mom had cancer, and Agnes was one of the few people who could comfort her. They shared jokes and stories of their lives with each other. Agnes was kind and funny, and made Mom laugh.

Agnes had a family – all grown up and even had six grandchildren and three great grandchildren. She married late in life and loved her husband as a true equal. Not long after her

31

first grandchild was born, her beloved Samuel died. After that, Agnes did not know what to do with her life. She always loved nursing. She always wanted to be a nurse, but it was never the right time to go back to school. Then, it was the right time. Agnes was on the dean's list and received her RN at the ripe older age of fifty-eight years old.

Agnes had a boyfriend now. Bryan was a little older than her, but he had a great sense of humor and style. He always kept her in a great mood. Bryan didn't work, as he was hurt on his job years ago, and had received disability, and now Medicare for many years. He lived with his daughter and grandchildren. As short and fat as Agnes was, Bryan was very tall and skinny as a stick. They looked really funny together – but very cute. Sometimes they both came for Sunday supper.

Chapter 12

Paul and Joe

Paul (Pablo) and his younger brother Joe (José) occupied a good-size unit on the third floor. They had a full bath they shared, two small bedrooms, a good-size kitchenette, and, even a stacked washer and dryer. They paid more for their unit than many of the other roomers.

Paul was forty-two years old and his brother Joe was thirty-seven. They were both divorced for many years, and both had one child. Paul had a daughter twenty-one in college and just married. Joe's son was seventeen and a junior in high school. The brothers had always been close. Paul, five years older than Joe, always looked after his younger sibling. Their parents died when they were young teenagers, and both went to live together in foster homes for some years.

Joe had gotten into trouble when he was in his late teens and early twenties. He spent almost two and one-half years in jail for some drug trafficking, but he was straight as an arrow for almost sixteen years now. He had learned his lesson and now just wanted to work, spend time with his son, and of course his great brother Paul.

The guys dated from time to time but no relationship ever got serious. They both were really afraid of commitment. However, they both had loads of male and female friends and pals that they spent time with and cherished. The guys never brought dates back to their unit, as the major rule of the rooming house was 'no women or dates above the first floor.' The women could sit in the kitchen, have meals, and even cook in the kitchen and use the big dining room. They could even go anywhere on the first floor, porch, patio, etc. – but never, ever upstairs.

Joe was very sleek and handsome, but Paul was much more intelligent and responsible. He was good looking also, but he wasn't a pretty boy like his brother. Paul was usually more serious, and always organized their lives and actions. The guys worked very hard – both were in construction. Many times they worked overtime on weekends to make some extra money to help give their children a better life. They usually paid their rent early, so they did not forget. They were good guys.

The brothers sometimes made Spanish and especially Mexican dishes in the big kitchen, so Lucy and some of the other men could enjoy also. Lucy loved every kind of food. She loved – loved – loved good food – almost as much as sex. The guys also taught Lucy Mexican dancing and played magical Spanish melodies. Lucy always dressed up in her finest peasant dresses, with lots of makeup, and her magnificent jewelry. She danced with the brothers sometimes until the early morning hours. It was one of all their favorite times together.

It was finally found out that Paul was seeing a woman, Margo, for the last fifteen months. They were very much in love now and were planning to live together in the near future. Margo had a good-size house and only one of her children was still living at home. Paul was going to move in with Margo, but his unit with Joe wasn't going to be empty. Paul and Joe's cousin Eric, who was in graduate school, wanted to move into Paul's part of the two bedroom unit. Lucy was overjoyed that she didn't have to look for another roomer. And the cousins were also very close.

The Gentlemen's Rooming House

Chapter 13

Isaac

Isaac was a Chinese-American gentleman in his mid-to-late forties. He had a slight build and was almost dainty–like in his stature. He was small and thin. He was very quiet and hardly spoke much English, even though he was born in America. He lived with his Chinese-speaking parents for most of his life until they died almost a year ago. He was extremely conservative and dressed as such. He wore dark, or mostly all black clothes, and always wore a black cap. He also carried a black briefcase. When his parents died, Isaac was all alone in the world, and wound up in a homeless shelter. After a while, he was more lonely than ever, and started to look for a more suitable residence. After looking through the newspapers, and talking to some people, he found Lucy's rooming house.

He also found the job he had now, as a cook and service waiter in a small but excellent Chinese restaurant. He worked in town – some fourteen miles away from the rooming house.

Isaac walked the one and one-half miles to the bus that he rode to work five days a week.

Isaac hardly ever took off his black wool hat, and always held tight his gray-black metal briefcase close to his chest. No one really knew what was in the briefcase, but no one ever asked – not ever. He was a very private person, and always seemed to have a mysterious past – or some big secret somewhere hidden in his head, his heart, or in his briefcase.

Isaac often brought home to Lucy fresh fried rice and dumplings and egg rolls. She loved fresh egg rolls. He really was a kind and serious man whose soul touched all who knew him.

Isaac almost never smiled, but when he looked into your eyes the room lit up. Ezra was somewhat friendly with Isaac, and he believed that Isaac carried around photos, items his parents owned, and even mementos of his parents' lives. Ezra tried to befriend him slowly, hoping to win his trust and friendship. After some time, he invited Isaac for lunch or supper when they were both finished work. They shared cooking their specialties at Ezra's place which was bigger. Ezra made his soul food and Isaac made his famous Chinese specialties. Leon liked

Isaac also, as they were both gentle and very sensitive. They all liked simple things, but Ezra tried to bring stimulation and excitement into Isaac's life.

Lucy told Isaac about a new little Oriental church about ten miles away. She thought he might meet some new people and perhaps make a friend or two. Lucy knew there were no buses running on Sundays, so she got an idea. She found an ad in the local newspaper about a used bike for sale at a very cheap price. Lucy always had some spare money hidden around the house, so she purchased the bike for thirty dollars, which was in perfectly good shape. It was a surprise for Isaac, and he was pleasantly delighted. He just loved it, and it was blue – his mother's favorite color. He did go to the new church after that, and he met a nice, older Chinese woman named Kara. They were just friends, but they came from similar backgrounds and spoke the same Chinese dialect. Their families lived in the same region in China. What a coincidence! After that, Isaac was extremely grateful to Lucy for everything, and he even wore pure white clothing on Sundays after that – in honor of his new life.

Chapter 14

Andy

Andy was the youngest of the gentleman roomers. He was just twenty-three years old, and he was a beautiful young man, literally and figuratively. His face looked like a little boy – chubby, with rosy cheeks and red moist lips. You just wanted to kiss and hug him. He was quite short, five feet six inches tall and he was built like a young man also. He was slender but muscular, and he had a gait of a sleek sinewy cat. Andy had dark eyes, but they were filled with past hurts and emotional losses. He had a very short haircut like an old-fashion butch haircut – like a marine.

Andy was a gentleman, sweet and always polite; he had strength of character. He was bright, ambitious and nothing in the world was going to get in his way of succeeding. He had confidence exuding from every part of his body. He was going to achieve all his goals. Andy went to the University of Arizona in Tucson – about forty-five to fifty minutes away from Rio Rico. He was finishing up his senior year and was set to receive his BS by the end of the year. He was even given a partial (very good) scholarship by his employers at the manufacturing plant where he worked for the last four years. Andy went to school two evenings a week and every other Saturday for six hours. He worked full-time at a manufacturing plant about fifteen miles away from the big house. He was a full-time manager, and everyone at the plant loved and respected him. He was an extremely hard worker, and even came in on Sundays if there was extra work that had to be done. The company wanted to pay for him to get his MBA, and he was excited about that. He had a late start in life but was finally beginning to catch up.

Andy's mom died when he was nine years old and he missed her very much. His dad who died about four years after his mom, was an alcoholic, and was somewhat abusive to Andy. He didn't remember any affection or attention ever from his father – only bad mouthing and put-downs. Andy lived with his great-aunt until he was sixteen years of age, and then he decided to just leave his past behind him. His great-aunt was good to him, but she was getting very old and senile. Andy found out in the last two years that his great-aunt Sadie had died.

Andy also found out in the last year that he had a half-sister Annette. He did not know about her until she called him one day, after looking for him for over two years. Andy found out that his father had a two-year affair with another woman, Annette's mom, eighteen to nineteen years ago. Annette was just eighteen years old and had just finished high school. She was living with her aunt in Nogales, and was ecstatic to have found Andy.

Andy kind of took her under his wing, as they were the only two persons left in the family. Annette's mom died three years before. The sister and brother saw each other about once a week for lunch or supper, or even a movie when time allowed. As time went on, Andy and Annette became very close. There were each others only family.

The Gentlemen's Rooming House

Chapter 15

Marty

Marty was a sixty-two year old Jewish man, the cutest and funniest of all the gentlemen roomers.

His wife died of cancer almost twenty-five years ago, and he had one son. He never remarried, but had a fifty-five year old lady friend named Claire. He went to her house for supper three to four times a week and he slept over those nights. They had been together almost ten years. Neither one wanted to change their relationship or living arrangements.

Marty still worked as a cab driver for over seventeen years and, the job still suited him. He loved talking to people and was so kind. If someone rode with him and was short of money Marty would put his own money in to make the bill. However, his routine passengers often gave him big tips because they loved him so. They bought him presents, and he shared his love and his funny jokes.

Marty just made enough money for his rent, food, necessities, dating Claire, and most of all – his two grandsons. They were four and six years old, and were the greatest joy in Marty's life. He adored them and they adored him. He and Claire spent time with Marty's son and daughter-in-law, and especially the two grandsons. They visited them about three times a week – especially on Sundays. Marty's days off were Sunday and Monday. His family loved Claire because she truly loved Marty, and took good care of him.

Marty was a fit and a very handsome man. He always dressed to the hilt. He wore tight shirts and even tighter jeans or trousers. He did not have more than and inch of body fat, and he worked out almost every morning before work. He usually wore a gold Chai necklace along with two other gold necklaces around his neck every day. Chai stands for *life* in Hebrew.

Marty and Lucy shared a flirty but very appropriate and friendly relationship. He always complimented Lucy with her clothes and beautiful figure, etc. Marty was the only roomer who could make Lucy blush. They just kidded around. Lucy always loved the way Marty smelled so good.

During the Jewish holidays, Claire and Marty would cook Jewish food in the big kitchen of the rooming house. Anyone who wanted to attend and celebrate also was invited. For big dinners on Sundays and for holidays, the roomers and their friends just paid a small fee for meals.

The Gentlemen's Rooming House

Chapter 16

Claire

Marty's lady Claire never married and had no children. She was a buyer for the major department store in the area some miles away and where she lived also. She was fit, pretty, smart, and very kind. She loved people and always tried to help them whenever she could. Claire and Lucy loved each other. She was also friendly with the other gentlemen roomers. Claire had the same job for over twenty-three years. It made her feel important, and, she loved fashion. Sometimes she took Lucy shopping in her department store and Lucy received a big discount. Claire usually picked her up.

Claire was also a confidante to Lucy when Lucy needed advice. Lucy respected Claire. They shared stories, jokes and especially tales of woe involving their pain and suffering with similar ailments. Claire had severe RA or rheumatoid arthritis. Claire had severe arthritis in her fingers which were bent, in her hands, hips and legs. Lucy had her severe fibromyalgia all over her body with eighteen points of pain.

Chapter 17

Omar

The newest roomer in the big house was Omar, a forty-two year old six foot three inch gentleman with dark black hair and very tan skin. His physique was statuesque to say the least. His dark brown eyes held thick eyelashes which made him look a bit ominous and held much mystery. He had a short nicely trimmed beard with white flecks running through the very black hair. His beard made him look very distinguished, and a bit older than his years. He dressed in the American way; he was always stylish and impeccably groomed.

Omar's parents died three years after they came to America. They took a tour bus from Rio Rico to the Grand Canyon, and the bus overturned on a slick ice covered curve on the highway. Omar had no living relatives in America, only a few cousins still in Israel.

Omar's grandparents lived in an Arab friendly area in Israel, but were killed in an Arab terror attack. What a cultural mess. Omar's father was only a very little boy when he was taken to an orphanage nearby, and after thirteen months, he was adopted by a Jewish couple. They had one other child who was also an orphan, but who was Israeli. Omar's father, Anua, grew up in a loving Jewish home and adopted all Jewish customs and traditions. He could speak fluent Hebrew also. He loved his adoptive parents and brother, and the family remained very close. Years later Anua married Omar's mom, Georgia, and then Omar was born.

Omar worked as a manager of a medium-size men's clothing store in Nogales, Arizona – very near Rio Rico. He had been there for seven years, and he really enjoyed his work. He had learned Spanish, and now he spoke English, Hebrew and Spanish. He was a college graduate; he was very smart but also very wise. He attended business college at night so he could obtain his master's degree. He was almost ready to graduate in a few months and receive his MBA. He was also saving as much money as possible to buy his own business in the future. He loved menswear, he loved the customers, he loved business, and he loved being independent. He wanted to open the same kind of store in Rio Rico, which definitely needed more upscale shops and businesses.

Omar was Jewish, however, he was taken for an Arab most of the time because of his name. He celebrated all things Jewish, and he became best friends with Marty, the other Jewish roomer. They often went out for a evening of fun, and they would do anything for each other.

Omar dated at times but no one was special in his life. He did work with a woman in the store who became a good, good friend. She was older, but very attractive, kind and smart. She was the one who taught Omar Spanish. They were never intimate, but they shared meals, movies and holidays together. Her name was Carmen, and she was a widow. She also had a daughter eighteen who was graduating high school. Omar sometimes invited Carmen for supper at the big house.

The Gentlemen's Rooming House

Chapter 18

James and Roger

James was sixty years old and was a part time writer for the local newspaper. He also substituted in middle and high school, and tutored some of the students. With everything, he earned just enough money to get by – and keep pretty busy.

James was very liberal and dressed as such. He never wore clothes that matched. He was six feet four inches and was very lean. He never ate meat; he only ate fruit and vegetables, herbs, dairy and whole grains. And, he only ate when he was very hungry. He always said Americans were very gluttonous creatures. They were greedy with their food and their possessions. James would wear a red tie, a blue shirt and pink sneaks. He looked like a real character, and, he certainly was one. But no one ever questioned his intelligence, and he certainly let everyone know about all his knowledge. James was a complete loner with everyone else except Roger – his partner and roommate. He had no real family except for Roger. He ran away from home when he was sixteen years old and never looked back. His parents were alcoholics and he had heard that they died some eleven years ago. He had no sibling. James was a very strict athlete. He ran every morning for one and one-half hours. He also went to a gym (his only treat) four times a week, and worked out vigorously.

James walked a narrow line – he was very decisive, very opinionated, and very sure of himself. He had some big ego. James gave all of his love, his affection, and his attention to Roger, his partner of twelve years. They met at a lecture given at a nearby community center. James's day began and ended with Roger. He was the love of his life. James only had one other mate in his life, and he lived with him over fourteen years. His name was Alex and he died in a drowning accident.

Roger was fifty years old. He was short and chubby. James and Roger together looked like Mutt and Jeff or resembled the story of Jack Spratt and his wife. Roger loved to eat anything delicious. He tried really hard to eat like James and watch himself, however, the pounds never came off. He would cry if he couldn't eat that luscious pizza or that juicy cherry pie. They both had their own little refrigerator. They shared a large one bedroom, full bath and small kitchenette on the third floor. Roger hated exercise but tried to go to the gym at least once a week. His pants always fell down, and his socks never stayed up. Roger was very street smart, and always had a smile on his face. He was the manager of a very large warehouse unit, where they stored everything for bedrooms. There were beds, mattresses, toppers, linens, bed frames, lamps, small tables and even bed posts. He worked there fifteen years and he made more money than James. Roger was married before and he had a son Nathan. Nathan was now eighteen years old and just graduated from high school. Roger really loved his son and saw him once every week for lunch or dinner, or just to go to the movies. Nathan's mother had a huge disgust for Roger, and for years did not allow Roger to see Nathan. Things were different now, as Natie was an adult. Roger found out that he preferred men when he was still married to his ex-wife Amy.

Amy, his ex, had remarried after the divorce, and later she forgave Roger and accepted him as he was. Amy and her new husband raised Nathan well, and years later the three parents became close friends – mainly for the benefit of Nathan's well-being.

Nathan was starting college after graduation. He was a great student and received a partial scholarship. Nate's stepfather had a lot more money than Roger, so he was willing to pay for most of his tuition. Roger really appreciated that gesture. Roger gave Natie spending money – as much as he could – every week, and Natie worked in the college bookstore for extra money for books and his computer software. There were also extra fees to be paid. Nathan still lived at home, as it was much cheaper that way. The college was only eighteen miles from his home.

Nathan loved Roger very much – but never really understood what made his father tick. He hoped that one day he could get close enough to him that he could get a lot of questions answered.

Chapter 19

Ezra

Ezra was an African-American man sixty years of age. He was Leon's dad and they lived together in a unit attached to the huge garage next to the house. In the garage was a huge storage unit for supplies, and there were three or four cars in the parking area. The men shared two small bedrooms, a full bath and a good-size kitchenette, as Ezra loved to cook. There was also a small laundry room.

Ezra was a very big man – very tall, broad, big belly and just very large. His belt was always so low trying to hold up his pot belly. His pure white teeth, his sad but sparkling green eyes, his wonderful smell – all made up kind and sincere Ezra. People all over loved Ezra. He always was a hopeful soul. He treated his son Leon so well – he took care of him – trained and mentored him, and loved him both as a mother and a father. Ezra never said a bad word about anyone or anything. Ezra was always spotlessly dressed and pressed. He pressed everything he ever wore – even his socks. Ezra knew a lot of people in the neighborhood, as he was a bus driver for twenty-seven years. He treated Lucy, her mom, and everyone else he ever met with respect and a great sense of humor. His hair was almost all white and brushed short. His hands were huge, as if to hold up the world. His shirts were starched – they could stand up on their own. His shoes were shined mirror bright.

Ezra was once married, but his beloved Mary died from untreated pneumonia two years after Leon was born. She died after twelve days in the hospital.

Ezra loved to read, and constantly held a newspaper in one hand and a Bible in the other. He always said words were everything. He read voraciously and always prayed a lot. He took Leon to church a couple of times a month. Transportation was hard to manage on Sundays.

Ezra sat with Mom for hours sometimes reading to her and talking about old times and how things were totally different now. Ezra grew some vegetables and even flowers outside the garage area. He often brought vegetables to Lucy and flowers to Mom. He also was in charge of firewood. Lucy gave him money to purchase the wood, and Ezra chopped it and made sure there was enough for warm firesides for the big house in the wintertime.

Chapter 20

Leon

Ezra's son Leon was a forty year old very immature man. He was a spitting image of his dad Ezra. He was round, clean-cut, and very well groomed. But, he didn't have the smarts or decision making of his dad. Unfortunately he was mentally challenged at an early age. And, he was socially deprived. He never married or dated, and he only had a few friends in his life. He did however go everywhere with his dad, and met people that way. He got along pretty well with the roomers.

Leon did work however in the large supermarket eleven miles from the house. He worked there for nine years as a bag packer, and recently was advanced to unpacking boxes, and refilling the shelves with groceries and canned goods. He was always on time, almost never got sick, and only missed two days of work in the last two years.

Leon loved his father Ezra and vice-versa. Ezra protected Leon at all expense. They helped each other with everything. Ezra cooked and cleaned and Leon did all the laundry and shined their shoes. They both loved shiny black shoes.

Leon and Ezra occupied part of a very large garage semi-attached to the big house. They had two small bedrooms, a full bathroom, a good-size kitchenette, and even a small laundry room. The garage was huge. Their unit was finished off like an apartment and the remainder of the separated garage was used for storage space for things and food for the big house.

Leon made enough money to help Ezra with the rent, to help pay for his clothes, necessities and some groceries. Leon also paid toward pizza night. He was very adamant about pizza every Friday night and always paid for most of the bill. That made him feel very important.

Leon rode his bicycle to work everyday, and the manager allowed him to keep it locked up in the back room while he worked all day. He worked diligently for five and one-half days a week, eight hours during each week day and half a day on Saturday. He was very proud of his work. Ezra worked five full days and worked four hours on Saturday morning to clean up some of the buses in the bus station.

Leon had two friends at the supermarket, and sometimes went to the movies with them on weekends. He loved the movies. He felt like he was with all the actors on the big screen. Leon also went to the park with Ezra in the evenings or on Saturdays. Leon loved the fresh air and the sounds of nature. He felt safe being close to the trees and the birds. They would bring their lunch and eat on one of the park benches.

Their apartment together was always spotless. Lucy loved the pair and they cared about her – and her mom. These men as well as all of the other roomers could use the big house, the sun-room, the outside porch and patio areas whenever they wanted – and at anytime, for the most part.

Lucy could always smell Ezra cooking ham hocks and collard greens. The aromas were so potent that Lucy could smell them even from the big house across the way.

The Gentlemen's Rooming House

Chapter 21

Lucy and Fibro

Beautiful Lucy had a debilitating disease known as the fibro syndrome. It involves over-active nerves, muscles and joints. One has a number of pressure points in the body, so when a physician tests for the disease, he touches or presses these points to see whether it evokes acute pain or soreness. A patient can have up to eighteen pressure points of pain. Twenty percent of the population, mostly women, experience chronic muscle, tendon and ligament pain, fatigue and multiple tender points on the body.

Lucy had suffered with fibromyalgia for about twelve years. They say that fibro occurs after a severe injury or shock to the system, and Lucy believed she got it right after the death of her fiancé Jake. That whole scene absolutely tore her apart. Lucy hurt all over her body, and she was told by her doctor that she had all eighteen pressure points. Sometimes, if someone bumped into her by accident, she would scream.

Besides the fibro, Lucy had other debilitating ailments related to the syndrome. She couldn't sleep well. She had a loss of good stabilizing balance, digestive issues, constipation and lack of concentration. She also suffered from extreme fatigue. She had a great many issues to overcome – but she managed very well. She exercised and walked everyday. She had come to love oriental meditation and chi kung. Also, she practiced tai chi and received two shiatsu massages a month. When the pain became too bad, Lucy had to lie in bed for three or four hours at a time. Sometimes the gentlemen roomers would help out with some chores, and she was forever grateful. When she felt good, she would be on her feet for eight to ten hours a day. She did a very excellent job of running the household, and also managing the men. She was always comforting the roomers with their problems and concerns. She was a great listener, and when the day ended, they all comforted her too.

Chapter 22

Lucy and Her Romances

Lucy was a virgin until the age of twenty years old when she was in college. She always read romance novels, and explored great love scenes in her mind and in her dreams. She was attached to several young men in and after college, but they were only casual sexual encounters, or short-term relationships. She was still in touch with a few of these men who remained friends even after her relationship and engagement to Jake. Lucy needed love, intimacy, and had a tortuous need for sexual fulfillment. She loved to hug and cuddle. She had two or so old flames that she saw at times, and that somewhat satisfied her needs.

One of these guys was Perry, who was a professor at a nearby community college. He was fifty-one years old, six feet two inches tall, and slim and had a good full head of hair. Hair and teeth were very important to Lucy. He always wore shiny shoes and argyle socks. He also always wore a bow tie and a velveteen vest. Perry was divorced for almost twenty-three years. His children were definitely grown and lived all over the country. He was only close to one of his children – his son Thomas. He wasn't a good father now or ever. And, he only saw Thomas once or twice a year. He really didn't care much about his few grandchildren. Perry was a man about town and essentially cared mainly for Perry. He also loved women, cigars, good whiskey and tennis. He loved going places like the opera, theater, good restaurants, and special parties and vacations. He was kind of a playboy. Perry had lots of friends who constantly invited him everywhere – parties, trips, fancy villas, horse shows and special openings.

Lucy liked going out with Perry very much. He dressed well, was charming, he knew almost everyone in Rio Rico or even in Tucson for that matter. He also loved beautiful and sophisticated Lucy on his arm. Everyone who was anyone knew Lucy also. He admired her confident presence, her individual style and her smarts. She loved being shown off, but sometimes it became too phony. Lucy loved real! Her pain and fatigue always was able to humble her. She had to always keep her feet on solid ground.

Perry was a handsome devil and he knew it. His one drawback in life was his bad leg. He limped a great deal as a result from a skiing accident years before. He was self conscious of his bad leg, but did walk with a most ornate 14K gold and black enamel walking stick which made the public gaze at his ornamental accessory rather than his deformity.

Lucy's other sometimes lover was Lenny. Lenny was always available to Lucy, but this one she had to hold back – otherwise he would be at the house all the time. Lenny was about the same age as Lucy, about thirty-seven or thirty-eight years old. He wasn't as handsome as Perry, and he was somewhat chubby. However, he absolutely adored Lucy, and he would be at her beck and call when she called him or needed him.

Lenny was married, but not very happily. He was a vice president in his father-in-law's manufacturing plant in Nogales, Sonora. He hated his job and he hated the situation he was in. His wife came from an ultra-wealthy family, and she was used to a variety of treasures in her life. She was a good person, but a very spoiled one. Lenny was cute and sweet, and always tried to please his wife. However he had almost become her boy toy, as she was twelve years older than him. She took advantage of his easy good nature, and was never satisfied with anything he did.

They were just a couple in name only. They both went out on their own, and only appeared together when there was a family function, or for public events. They had one child – a daughter twelve years of age. They were married almost thirteen years now. Lenny just loved – loved – loved his daughter Ally, and he spent as much time as possible doing things with her. Lenny was a good and hard working man, and he tried to keep the peace at home and at the plant. And, Lenny didn't know that his wife Marge was having affairs with two of the richest men at the country club. He was so good, that he did not have a clue about his wife's escapades.

Lenny met Lucy at the big food market nearby, when they both tried to get in line to check out. He noticed her sparkling personality and her springy step. She had a quirky attitude with her fun smile as their grocery carts bumped into each other on purpose. That was the beginning of a very special friendship and more.

Lucy cared about him a great deal, but never expected anything serious. He loved his daughter Ally, and it turned out that at the age of nine, she was diagnosed with acute lymphocytic leukemia. Lenny took Ally to the hospital in Tucson two times a month for radiation treatments. The hospital was specifically for children and young adults with cancer – especially leukemia. Lenny's wife Margo became too nervous to face Ally's hospital visits, so Lenny took all the responsibility.

Lenny was enthralled with Lucy's wonderful character, and he really needed more from her. However, Lenny was only a good friend to Lucy, and she made that clear to him.

David was a forty-five year old military software genius. He came to Rio Rico four times a year for four or five weeks at a time. He fell in love with Rio Rico after a visit, and, he fell in love with Lucy as well. He had an incredible smile with perfect teeth which Lucy absolutely loved. He was stocky but rugged looking, and he was very sensual. David and Lucy hit it off when they first met, and they romanced each other every time he stayed in Rio Rico at the big house. David was married and was a father to two boys. He was not happily married but did not divorce for the sake of the boys.

They had plenty of fun together, and Lucy loved sharing poetry and literature, music and art – all of it with David. They also went to plays and movies, but when David had to leave town,

Lucy always grieved. Lucy and David's love affair was just part time and Lucy needed more.

Chapter 23

Shiatsu and Louie

It was a very cool Tuesday morning in January and Lucy was feeling a bit tired and achy.

She dreaded the cold and was almost tempted to grab the blankets on the bed and re-snuggle herself under the covers. She loved the sunshine and its warmth – but it was kind of bleary outside – like the weather up north. She went into the living-dining room and lit a fire in the marble fireplace. She relaxed before the fire in her robe and jammies. Oh, the warmth hugged her muscles and bones. In a few minutes she was ready to take on the day.

An hour later Agnes came in to take care of Mom, the washing machine was running, the dryer was buzzing, and Lucy was in her office already paying bills.

Ezra popped in to tell Lucy that Leon was home sick, and asked her to please check in on him – if she could. Ezra did not want to miss work – he needed the money.

73

Lucy did her morning chores and got dressed. She wore a bright pink outfit today to help offset the bleary weather. She had to go out for her afternoon appointment with her shiatsu healer for a massage. The massage made her feel much more poised, relaxed and focused. During the massage treatment, Louie, that was his name, just happened to brush too close to Lucy, and his hand just happened to slide up her leg and pressed her personal area. Lucy shivered a bit and thought he was just working very closely on her meridians. However, after he requested that she take off her leggings to work closer on her pulse points she refused and composed herself. He knew that she always wore loose clothes when receiving a shiatsu massage. So she knew that he was playing dirty with her. Louie had almost always flirted with Lucy, and he did go over the line when he hugged her hello and goodbye; however, this was just inappropriate and improper behavior for a massage healer. Lucy told Louie that he was definitely out of line and that she would not be coming back. Before she left she took the honor of slapping his face as hard as she could, and slamming the door behind her. Whew! What a jerk he had become!

Lucy returned home flushed and very upset. Louie had always been her favorite massage healer – now she would have to look for someone else. What a drag, she thought. She calmed down and took some deep breaths. She stopped in to see if Leon needed anything, but he said he was doing a little better. Just hugging Leon and seeing him in his giant nightshirt and big hat made Lucy smile and made her feel much lighter. Leon knew how to take his aspirin that Ezra left for him, and he was drinking a lot of orange juice like Lucy said. Lucy felt better after she spoke to Leon, and she knew she had to break off ties with Louie. It was much too stressful. Tomorrow she would call around for another practitioner.

The Gentlemen's Rooming House

Chapter 24

Sun You are my Friend

Lucy loved the sunshine and the sun returned her love. She usually wore sunscreen in the summer especially, but her skin still became rosy pink and eventually somewhat tan. She tried to walk at least four to five times a week, as it always helped alleviate stiffness and muscle pain. She even wrote poetry about the sun and how it brightened her life.

When the sun kissed her skin and body, the embers of the heat also fired up her sexual prowess. Besides the vitamin and relaxation benefits, the sun made her feel alive, happy and inflamed with desire.

Lucy was a rare breed of a woman. She could control her pelvic muscles in such a way that she could climax just when the sun pressed on her private areas.

Even when she was a young girl in school, she could alleviate stress during an exam by controlling her pelvic muscles, and even reach a light climax.

When it rained in Arizona, which was almost never, Lucy had a sunlamp.

Oh Sun

I celebrate your awakening every day, for you are truly my closest friend!

Your hot embers penetrate my soul and blanket it with peace.

You deliver my mind from troubled thoughts - you are my friend!

Your hands reach out and envelop my flesh with renewed joy and awakening.

You feed me from your mouth 'til I am satiated with energizing strength.

When you disappear from my eyes, I can still feel your spirit within me.

What more can I ask from a friend?

You are close, and yet I share you with so many.

Your love shines on only me, and then you reach out like a fickle suitor and share with all.

I love you Sun - I love your happy smile.

I need you Sun - I need your intimate hands.

I respect you Sun - I respect your infinite years.

Oh Sun - you are truly my friend!

Chapter 25

The Weather
and
Lazy Day Talk

Most people don't become overly anxious about the weather, but people in Southern Arizona do. The oppressive dry heat can wipe anyone out if they are outside too long. Sometimes in the summer months the temperature can top one hundred and ten degrees. Rio Rico was somewhat cooler than say Scottsdale or Phoenix, but it was still blasted hot. In the winter or spring months Lucy would walk everyday for exercise and better digestion. With fibromyalgia, Lucy almost always was constipated and suffered with stomach pain and bloating. The walking helped the food go down.

Also, in Arizona, people would have to drink a massive amount of water if they wanted to stay hydrated. People would pass out all the time from the heat and dehydration.

In the tepid breezy days of November to May, Lucy and Mom spent wonderful days outside talking and joking around about their lives. Lucy, could tell Mom anything and everything. They shared love stories, jokes, hopes, dreams and hurtful memories of pain and

81

loss. From these stories of the past, Lucy found out a lot about Mom's single life before Dad. Lucy didn't know that Mom had a very active sex life like Lucy. Wow. Mom told Lucy she once reached ten orgasms in one night. Lucy told Mom she topped her with eighteen orgasms in one night. The ladies laughed. It was wonderful that a daughter could share such information with her mother. The two were close.

Sometimes Lucy would wheel her Mom in the wheelchair around the property. Mom loved to hear the birds sing and take in all the smells of the season's flora.

The cats would occasionally come outside to frolic in the sunshine. They would romp around on their backs and lick themselves to pieces. They could not stay outside too long or they would run away too far. Those were glorious days.

Chapter 26

Trip to Nogales, Mexico

It was summertime and very cloudy. Lucy had never slept with any other roomers except David, when he came to Arizona for intervals of his work. However, on a brief trip to Nogales, Mexico, Paul took Lucy shopping when he went to visit some friends. Lucy spoke some Spanish, and she really enjoyed the playful banter of the merchants, and, the special items that she could only buy in that area.

Later in the day after both had done whatever they had to do, a dangerous monsoon started up, and the rain and wind had overcome the streets of Nogales. The two had to remain in the car parked in a partially closed lot for almost four hours. It was scary for Lucy, as she always feared storms – especially with the great noise and lightning.

It was tight quarters in the car, and after two or three hours in a heated parked car their bodies seemed to touch more and more, and before they knew it, they were rubbing and kissing each other. They didn't even look at each other, as they undid their clothes. They had a wild time during sex but it was a true quicky. Afterward, they still didn't look at each other, but they quickly dressed and Lucy told Paul that this sexual encounter would never happen again, and that neither one of them would ever talk about it. Paul agreed and told her he was truly sorry. Lucy said she was to blame also.

Lucy felt betrayed by herself. She broke her own rules about sleeping with the roomers. David was different – he came only several times a year, and he was really her friend and lover. And, there was true love and kinship with David. He was her equal. She told herself she was really naughty but she would get over it. He did have a fabulous body!

This incident did not take place after she met Esteban. It was way before – almost eight months before.

Chapter 27

Esteban

As the day began, Lucy received a phone call from Andy who asked if he could bring his best friend to dinner the next evening, and he also wanted Lucy to meet him. His name was Esteban. Lucy wondered who was this man that Andy wanted her to meet. She was a bit excited.

The next evening Andy brought his friend home for supper. When Lucy's eyes sought out this new stranger in her home, she felt a rather new and wondrous sensation in her heart. She felt a heartbeat in her body that she never felt before. She couldn't breathe well, and her stomach tightened up as in orgasm. His name was Esteban – Steven. He was Andy's best friend, and he was Andy's teacher. He was very tall and well built – but he definitely had meat on his bones – and a small pouch of a stomach sticking out. He dressed well – kind of preppy.

He had on argyle socks, black shined loafers, a blue button-down shirt and khaki trousers. He also wore a grey suede sports jacket. He looked like he just came out of a fashion magazine.

Esteban's face was round with high cheek bones and big lips. His nose was straight and regal. His hair was reddish-brown, very straight, and fell down all over his eyes. He looked impish. Oh, and by the way – Esteban wore braces. He was a big, little boy.

Andy introduced Esteban as his best friend and, also one of his professors. Wow, so young and so mature – and, so handsome! When Lucy shook Esteban's hand, she felt sparks all the way up to her nipples. They were sticking out like very pointed pencils. Lucy asked Andy how old Esteban was – and he told her old enough. They both giggled and he said late twenties. That evening, that day, that meeting would change Lucy's life forever.

After supper, Lucy, Andy and Esteban sat in the living room / dining room and the talk began. Lucy had so many questions to ask Esteban and she bubbled with excitement. She couldn't get too excited – as even very good emotions and feelings sometimes acted like severe stress in her body, and she would start to hurt. Her body was so vulnerable to everything going on in her life.

Lucy found out that Esteban was single, no children, never married and he had a masters degree, and, was working on his doctorate. G-d, Lucy was so proud of him – she couldn't believe what he had accomplished at such a young age. So handsome, so smart, so sexy, so sweet and so young! Lucy was getting more and more excited as she learned more and more about Esteban. Before he left that night, Lucy showed him around the big house and the property. Little did Lucy know that on the other end Esteban was also totally impressed by, and smitten with her. It would be a while until the two would meet again.

The Gentlemen's Rooming House

Chapter 28

The First Meeting

The night Lucy met Esteban with Andy proved to be a most unsettling experience. Lucy felt happy and excited, but also felt confused and a little bit sad. Why was she so sad – she didn't really know or understand. She was attracted to his body, his entire presence, his smarts, his class. She liked all that – but could she really be interested in such a young man? He looked so young – so innocent – and oh my G-d – he even wore braces. Lucy found out that Esteban was twenty-six years old, very mature, very responsible, and very passionate about life and learning. He lived in nearby Nogales, Arizona, but taught at the University of Arizona in Tucson. He felt his doctorate degree was taking forever.

Little did Lucy know that Esteban was also feeling happy but confused. He believed that Lucy was the most gorgeous creature he had ever seen. He wondered if he had a chance with her because she was so sophisticated and charming.

Oh well, they would both see what would happen.

The Gentlemen's Rooming House

Chapter 29

Sundays

Sunday was the only day of the week where the roomers or family could bring a guest – even women to the house. Sunday was also the only day of the week where dinners were served in the main dining room. Martha, the part-time cook made simply fantastic meals all completely homemade. She energized herself every weekend to show off her culinary skills, and great aptitude for decorating. She had a different theme every Sunday and made special ethnic delicacies to match the theme of the day. The meals only cost five dollars and ninety-five cents and the roomers and especially their guests absolutely loved and savored those meals. Most Sundays however, Martha made roast beef, chicken, or even barbequed steaks as the main dish. There was a large gas barbeque outside of the kitchen area where even the roomers could grill whenever they desired. Martha's deserts were totally rich, elegant and very fattening. There was apple pie, different flavors of parfaits, éclairs, puddings, flan and Italian ices.

Martha did not make much money as a part-time cook. Since the suppers were so reasonable, the roomers and guests each Sunday would leave extra money for her, as a tip. They all gave whatever they could afford because they appreciated her work. However, Lucy was the one who charged only a limited fee of five dollars and ninety-five cents a dinner, and she paid for all of the food herself. The roomers were aware of this wonderful gesture of Lucy's, and whenever she needed help, they were always there for her.

Most Sundays there were at least ten to twelve people at the big table in the living-dining area. Sometimes Lucy had an amateur singer or musician come in on a Sunday to entertain the roomers and guests. Lucy loved making people happy, and she loved cheery festivities. Even Mom came downstairs sometimes to enjoy the fun. But as Mom always said, "No guests above the first floor!"

Lucy was going to invite Esteban next Sunday for supper, and she was going to introduce him to the roomers. What a great idea! She would see how everyone reacted to him as Lucy's guest and friend.

Chapter 30

First Date
Dinner with Esteban

Two days and six hours after Lucy first met Esteban, he called to ask her if he could take her out for dinner. She thought for two seconds and said, "Sure."

He picked her up the next evening at 6:30PM, and he brought her a beautiful red flowering plant. She was happy it wasn't flowers, as a flowering plant would certainly live longer. Lucy just loved the gesture and intimately felt that Esteban was trying to impress her. She really liked him a lot and didn't even know him that long. However, by the end of the long evening the two had become quite close. She felt like a school girl, and for some reason, she loved the protective and gentlemanly behavior he showed her. He seemed so mature, so confident, and yet so humble. And yet she knew he was so much younger than her, and, he wore braces! The two of them had a marvelous supper and even went out for a little music, and one drink at a nearby pub. Neither one wanted the evening to end, but by 1:00AM they both hugged and in an instant

Esteban pulled her to him and gave her a brief but intense kiss. She rocked for a minute – then got her bearings. They bid farewell for now.

However, one half-hour after the farewell kiss and as Lucy was getting ready for bed, the phone rang. It was Esteban! He wanted to check on Lucy, and told her that his heart was filled with joy after the date. Lucy laughed out loud, even though no one could hear her except Esteban. She told him she felt the same way, but she had reservations because of their age difference. Esteban laughed and told her the age difference was nothing, and that their feelings meant everything. Lucy asked him how old he really was, and he said twenty-six years old – which was really not the late twenties as he first said. He was thirteen years younger than her. Lucy sighed from confusion and happiness – both at the same time. She felt so right with Esteban. He said all the right things! He was so much fun – yet so deep and mature. Lucy said her final good night, and she comforted herself among all the blankets on the bed. She slept well that night and dreamed about Esteban.

Chapter 31

The Second Date and After That

Two days after Lucy and Esteban had their first date, he called and told her he wanted to take her to Phoenix to hear a concert with the group *Il Divo*. Andy had told Esteban that Lucy loved the group, and he heard they were coming to Arizona. So, he bought two tickets really fast, as he wanted to take her to hear her favorite group. She was extremely excited about the concert and her new special friend.

The concert was a huge success, and Lucy felt so happy and so adored. When they returned home it was still early in the evening and Lucy asked Esteban if he would like to stay for supper. Lucy was going to cook. Esteban licked his lips, and told Lucy that she was a fantastic cook. He always complimented her on everything. What a good guy! She was slowly removing the doubt and worry about their age difference.

Later that week Esteban brought Lucy flowers, her mom a beautiful new blanket, and he took Lucy to the movies. Esteban came by every day at different times to see Lucy, and they kissed and hugged every time. By Sunday

95

evening Lucy asked him if he wanted to stay over. Esteban slowly shivered and said yes!

That night brought the two single people a bond that would not ever be broken. The ecstasy – the passion, and the reverence for each other was almost like a heavenly experience. They both climaxed multiple times, and the bed was very sweaty as a result. They both smiled and held each other for hours. Esteban left about 3:00AM as he had to be up very early – 6:00AM to be exact. He left with his shoes in his hand. Lucy could not stop kissing him as he tried to leave. Five minutes later Esteban was gone, and Lucy was changing the linens.

Chapter 32

Meet His Parents

Esteban wanted Lucy to meet his parents, so they planned an evening visit for Friday night supper.

When Lucy came into their home, she was welcomed with great kindness and love. His parents were Roberta and Jaime (Haime). Roberta was tall and slim, very elegant and stately looking. She had long blonde hair tied back from her face in a simple ponytail. She had deep blue eyes and high cheek bones. Her smile was bright and fetching. Her teeth were white as snow, and her skin was tawny-colored and very smooth. She was dressed in a black and white jumpsuit, very modern and smart, looking. Gosh, she could pass for Esteban's older sister. Esteban's father was tall and slim also. He was very handsome and had thick brown-black hair cut very short. His hair was graying at the temples. No wonder Esteban was so attractive. His parents looked like Hollywood actors. Jaime wore a white silk long sleeve shirt and tight black silk trousers. His parents matched clothes – black and white.

Jaime and Roberta both hugged and kissed Lucy. Esteban cheered with delight. What a wonderful family. Esteban had no siblings either.

Lucy saw a very festive meal on the table with candlesticks. Roberta told Lucy that they were actually Jewish – and this was their Sabbath meal. She lit the candles and recited the prayers. She shut her eyes and waved her hands in front of her face. Lucy believed she never had seen anything so beautiful in her life. She also didn't know that Esteban was Jewish. The atmosphere was electric and ethereal. There was love and peace in that home that night.

When they were seated in the living room before supper, they drank their wine, and eyed each other with smiling hearts. Roberta began a story about their families and their ancestors who lived in Spain long ago – even before 1492. They were Jewish, but had to conceal their religion from the people, who were mostly Catholic and the government. Their ancestors had to practice Judaism privately and in hiding. They were known as Morano Jews. They had to make believe that they practiced Catholicism like the masses. However in 1492 the Jews were mostly found out and were exiled along with the

Moors from Spain. Many of the Jews immigrated to Portugal, and many immigrated to Turkey. Jaime and Roberta's families wound up in Portugal and many years later moved to America. All through the generations, the two families remained very close and loyal to each other. They always still practiced Judaism in private and with each other. They were so used to this kind of life that even when the two families moved to Arizona – and even to the present day – their Jewish beliefs were silent. Eventually the two families (great-grandparents) ended up in Rio Rico. Through the years they were leading doctors and dentists, teachers and business owners.

Esteban's parents fell in love since middle school. They went to college together and eventually married. They knew each other since they were toddlers. Esteban was the only child; Roberta could not have any more children. Esteban loved and respected his parents and they adored him. Jaime and Roberta were both CPAs and they worked together. They ran an office in Nogales and they were well known in the community.

Roberta told Lucy that they did not go to synagogue, but they still practiced all the Jewish traditions and customs – and celebrated all the holidays in private like their ancestors before them.

Lucy was fascinated and very interested in what she heard. She intended to learn more and perhaps even join in this practice. As time went by, she became enthralled with Judaism and even embraced the idea of conversion. Esteban, his parents, Judaism, their whole way of life. Wow – all of it inspired Lucy. She felt like she had a real family, and she wanted to be part of it. She felt an intimacy she had never felt before. It was good! It was going to get even better.

Chapter 33

Likes and Dislikes

Esteban and Lucy loved to do things together. They loved to sit outside on the white and green swing and swing and chat for hours. Sometimes they would take the cats outside to romp on the grassy patches.

They loved fresh summer fruit that was ripe and healthy. Esteban would peel the luscious peaches and nectarines, and Lucy would savor and devour each wet morsel until only a big dark pit was left.

They preferred the simple everyday things in life like breaking string beans and preparing them for supper.

They both enjoyed going to county fairs and amusement parks when they came to Phoenix or Tucson. They always tried to go to the Renaissance Fair and to the famous International Gem Show in Tucson. They also loved the circus and they liked to slow-dance to the oldies.

Lucy's love of art led them to art shows and museums - when they had time. They saw each other at least four or five times a week.

They took long walks around town and more and more people got to know them.

The couple enjoyed playing dress up games. At times they would dress formal and eat in the dining-room. They used their fancy sterling tableware, cloth napkins, gold dishes, a brocade damask tablecloth and Grandmom's polished brass candlesticks. They would also spend evenings role playing King and Queen of some far-off nation – sometimes stripping down to slave and master. They loved to have good fun together.

And most of all they loved each other and their families. Home-life was everything to them.

What they didn't like was laziness and phonies, macho people and scam-artists. They preferred real and good people who worked hard and raised good families.

Chapter 34

Fear and Empowerment

One evening Ezra and Leon came into the big house. They looked very pensive and troubled. Ezra asked to speak to Lucy about something serious. They all sat down and discussed the problem. Leon has been bullied at work. Everyone at work knew he was mentally challenged and treated him with dignity and respect. They all loved his kind and gentle ways. However, some neighborhood teenagers outside the market harassed him with bullying tactics – like bad names and threats. Leon was afraid to come outside during his lunch break. He was also afraid to walk home after work sometimes, as one or two of them often followed him.

Leon was not a coward, but the pressure of fear and anxiety started to cause an emotional breakdown. Lucy told Ezra that she was going to find a way to help Leon. She knew that if Ezra took the responsibility of approaching those boys he would surely hurt them or suffer a heart attack in the process.

The next few days Lucy thought about the situation and decided to talk to Isaac. He knew

103

martial arts, he was very strong and very effective. He could approach these boys as a slight figure of a man, but in reality he was a force to be reckoned with. Lucy met with Isaac and he agreed to pass by the food market and check out the guys that hung around.

Days later Isaac went one or two times a day for short periods of time casing the neighborhood. Finally, one day late in the afternoon he saw the boys. There were three of them.

One of them was short and chubby. The other two were thin and bony. All three had tattoos on their arms and necks. They were shabbily dressed and dirty-looking.

Isaac slowly approached them and asked if they knew a young man named Leon. They laughed at Isaac declaring their dislike of Leon. They called him a Wus. They said they went after him because he was a weakling and couldn't fight back. Isaac told the boys they had been wrong, because Isaac taught Leon some karate, and he would, and could fight back in the future. The boys were a bit confused at this little man telling them all this news. They almost didn't believe him, until he knocked all three boys down with swift but almost deadly karate kicks and movement. He knew both karate and kung fu. His favorite kung fu movements were *xuan zi* or butterfly kicks and *wing chun* front kicks. However, he only reserved these movements for strong opponents.

Chapter 35

Hot Showers and Sex

Lucy loved hot baths and showers. She only took showers when she was in a hurry or when she was accompanied by Esteban. Oh what fun it was when they took long showers together. He would gently wash her entire body – limb by limb. He would use a fluffy soft sponge soaked with Italian honey cream cleanser. It smelled earthy and fresh and it felt so, so good. Esteban made her body feel alive and her skin felt like silk. The hot shower helped to loosen up her muscles and it helped alleviate some of her pain. When they finished bathing, Esteban towel-dried Lucy with a huge plush Persian towel. The towel enveloped her small body with comforting warmth. He then laid her down on the king size bed in her bright yellow bedroom.

They both massaged each other with lavender and shea butter cream and oil, until they were seething with passion. On good days when Lucy felt good and she didn't hurt so much, they could come together in the most normal way. But when her health was bad, they both satisfied each other in every other way. They could climax multiple times in an evening. Esteban was not the biggest guy, but he was very strong and very enduring. And, they could kiss and embrace for hours. Their love was sensitive and gentle but also extremely sexual and ecstatic. When Lucy became too hot, Esteban would rub her entire body with ice cubes.

Chapter 36

Omar's Fire

Day's after Leon's ordeal with the three street kids ended, another problem emerged.

Omar had a terrible fire in his store. An employee was scheduled to open the store at 8:30AM that morning. However, when he had arrived at 8:15AM and started to open the front door, a rush of hot smoky air enveloped him. He could barely see through the smoke and hot embers. He quickly dialed 911 and moments later he dialed Omar. Andy was still at home when Omar received the bad news. He told Omar he wanted to help him, and the two guys left the house quickly.

When the two arrived at the store, the firemen were already there. The fire started in the back of the store. It took almost four hours to quell the fire and the money damage was almost $300,000. The electric wiring in the back of the building was very old – and some of the wires were threadbare.

The store was closed for six weeks, and then only the front of the store was open for customer business. Insurance did cover most of the cost of rebuilding and restoration after the fire, but some business was definitely lost. There was substantial economic loss.

After the fire, there was a small infestation of mice on the property, and Lucy allowed her three kitties to take part in ending that problem. It worked! The kitties did not really eat the mice, but they surely scared them away.

Four months after the fire, Omar had a grand reopening of the store with fifty percent newer fixtures, new walls and wall covers, new shelves, and, a great new paint job. After the opening, past customers as well as a great many new ones spent a good amount of money supporting Omar and the business. The Spanish brothers Paul and Joe spent all their free time helping Omar fix up the store for the grand reopening. Andy also helped on weekends.

Omar's boss was so impressed with Omar's work and devotion to save the business that he offered Omar an opportunity to buy the business and pay it out over ten years with very low interest. What a great opportunity for Omar. He didn't have the down payment that his boss had wanted, however, Lucy made an appointment for Omar to speak to her friend at the bank. The gentleman was very fond of Lucy, and he granted a loan to Omar for the down payment of the store. The banker also felt that the store would be a very fine investment.

Omar's boss was quite old and had no real family. He granted this great chance to Omar as he was always impressed with Omar's work ethic and dedication. He almost treated him like a son he never had.

The gentlemen roomers proved again that their friendship and support always paid off with good results.

Chapter 37

Stiffness and Pain

Wednesday morning Lucy awoke with great stiffness in her legs and shoulders. She remembered she had to find another shiatsu healer. Even her stomach hurt bad today. She had an appointment with a gastroenterologist for next week. Some days she just wanted to give up, but she knew she could never do that. She had too many people depending on her. So, she took some ibuprofen and headed to the kitchen to eat some soup.

Claire called Lucy and they planned on going shopping in Claire's department store that afternoon. Claire thought it would pick up Lucy's mood if she bought something new for herself. Claire told Lucy that bright colors were in fashion, and, Lucy picked out a bright hot pink short cardigan sweater with lace around the collar. Lucy loved feminine lace. Shopping always made Lucy feel young and spirited.

When Lucy returned home she rested for awhile and then practiced her meditation. She took very deep breathes to steady her racing mind. When she meditated today, she concentrated on visions of her deceased dad, and her fiancé Jake. She missed them both so much. But she ended her meditation with wholesome thankfulness.

When Lucy entered Mom's bedroom, she saw her standing up by the window and looking out at the bare and arid landscape. After all, it was the dead of winter and even Arizona had cold dreary days. The women hugged and Lucy sat Mom down to brush her very fine hair. It seemed that mom's hair, as well as her body was becoming thinner and weaker every day. Agnes then came in to resume her duties with Mom. Then Marty dropped in to say hello to the women. He was in between cab rides and came home briefly to grab some late lunch. Lucy spent the rest of the day paying bills and cooking some of her favorite dishes. She loved to cook and she loved to eat.

Before the day ended Lucy received a phone call from Perry. He proceeded to inform Lucy that he was through with women, and, he had found a spectacular male partner and lover. Oh well, Lucy just wished him good luck and smiled to herself. She wanted to laugh, but she hurt too much. He said he was off women, like he just gave up sweets!

114

Chapter 38

Lucy's Condition Gets Worse

Lucy woke up with a puddle of blood under and around her. She had her menstrual period but never experienced so much blood. Dr. Adams did tell her that excessive bleeding was a result of her multiple fibroid tumors. She yelled for Agnes to please come and help her. Fortunately, Agnes came in early that day and heard Lucy scream. She hurried to help Lucy who was crying with tears running down her cheeks. Lucy was very pale. She knew that heavy bleeding was expected but she hated the scary mess. She was a very clean and orderly woman. Agnes helped her remove her pajamas and guided her to the shower. Agnes then swept up all the heavily soiled linens and placed them in the washer.

Lucy showered and put on clean clothes for the day. She felt better after awhile, especially after splashing on some Chanel No. 5 perfume. The scent was fresh and sexy and always soothed Lucy's being. It also made her feel classy and elegant.

Lucy called Dr. Adams and made an appointment to see him in the next couple of days. She knew she could not go on with this bleeding, weakness and heavy pain.

She called Esteban – just to hear his voice. He was always so calm and positive. He was an old soul who just happened to wear braces. She also questioned herself again if Esteban was the right man for her. He was so young – she thought to herself – but such a great person! Oh well.

Chapter 39

Bad News

On Thursday morning Lucy awoke with a strange feeling in her heart – one of fear – mixed with a feeling of gratitude for living every day to the fullest. She meditated for over twenty minutes that day trying to relax, give thanks for her blessings, and also praying for positive results from the tests the day before. Lucy had a gnawing feeling that the news would not be very good.

Before leaving for the Dr., Lucy met Omar and Isaac in the dining room where they were eating oatmeal and fruit. She thought that meal really looked good, and she made more oatmeal and joined them for an early breakfast. The oatmeal warmed her innards, and she also loved sunflower seeds and sliced almonds in the big bowl. As good as it was, Lucy felt a feeling of dread in her belly. She was not expecting an easy day.

Lucy left early for her appointment with Dr. Adams. He looked very stern and austere that morning. Lucy sat down and the doc told her he had some bad news. First he told Lucy that she had twenty-two fibroid tumors, and also some bad looking disease in her ovaries. The fibroids didn't look cancerous, but they had to come out. They were causing great pain and extremely heavy menstrual periods. As far as the ovaries were concerned, Doc Adams believed she should have a complete hysterectomy. He hoped for no cancerous cells in her uterus, but he would not know until he operated and did the necessary tests. The doc also told Lucy she would not be able to have children after the operation. Lucy was shaking and almost passed out from shock. She took some deep breaths and Dr. Adams went around his desk to comfort her. She started crying and did not stop until she returned home.

Lucy was afraid to drive herself home, so she called Omar – who wasn't scheduled to go to work until 2:00PM. As it was only 10:15AM she called him to please help her get home. Andy drove her car home late that night with the help of Omar. Lucy continued to cry all the way home, and Omar didn't exactly know what to do. She burst out telling him she needed a complete hysterectomy and could never have children through childbirth. In the living room / dining room Agnes was bringing hot green tea to Mom, and Agnes noticed Lucy with tears flowing from her eyes. Agnes put down the tray and went to Lucy to hold her tight. She also heard Lucy tell Omar what bad news she had just received from Dr. Adams. Agnes held Lucy for a few minutes until she calmed down a bit. She told her she would be right down after bringing Mom her tea. Afterwards, she gave Lucy some orange-chamomile tea to soothe her. Lucy told them both that the surgery was scheduled for the following Thursday morning. Lucy said she didn't know how she would be able to handle the house and everything after the surgery. Omar and Agnes both reassured Lucy that everything would be taken care of. Lucy did not know what to think. Agnes told Lucy that she would stay over that night to take care of Mom and the house. She told Lucy to go upstairs and rest.

When Lucy woke up from her nap, she tried to settle down and get herself together. The phone rang right away, and it was Lenny. She wanted only good vibes from him, but he told her he could not see or help her anymore. He and his wife had a real awakening the other night. They declared their infidelities to each other, and his wife especially, was very apologetic for everything. They both agreed for the sake of family and the children that the infidelities were over. Lenny told Lucy that he would really miss her, however he had to save his marriage and his family – and of course his job at his father-in-law's giant operation. Lucy agreed to Lenny's decision and wished him good luck. That conversation just made her feel worse – she lost a good and loyal friend.

Chapter 40

Planning a Meeting

It was Friday night and Lucy decided to have a special delicious meal for this Sunday supper. She asked Martha to work a little overtime to cook and shop. She explained to Martha that she was not well and needed to have a big operation. Martha agreed to do whatever was needed, and she would work as many hours as possible when Lucy was hospitalized.

Lucy stopped in to see all the roomers on Friday and Saturday, to ask them to please attend the special Sunday supper this week. She told all the guys and the rest of the support staff that she had an important announcement to make. Lucy called Claire and asked her to please come on Sunday with Marty. Claire agreed and offered to help in any way.

By 6:00PM on Sunday all of the roomers were gathered in the living room / dining room area. Also, Claire, Martha, and Esteban were there right beside Lucy. Agnes helped Mom come downstairs, and, she was even dressed up in a lovely white caftan with a white shawl to cover her frail thin legs. Claire made the shawl

121

for Mom the year before. Claire was such a good woman. Mom's face was drawn with extra worry and sadness concerning Lucy's illness. Everyone hugged Mom with caring affection.

Lucy had everyone sit down. She then briefly, but candidly told about her upcoming surgery, and that she needed as much help and cooperation as possible. She broke up in tears toward the end of the speech. Everyone reached out to hug and reassure her fears.

They all started planning what each one would do. Martha said she would work overtime to have things in control. Agnes was going to take care of Mom staying over each night.

Ezra and Leon were going to keep the house and grounds in shape. Omar, Paul and Joe were going to plan a barbeque one evening, and they were going to pay for everything. Isaac was going to cook Chinese food one night, and he would take care of the cats. Claire and Esteban were going to accompany Lucy to the hospital on the scheduled date – and they intended to stay with her. All the other gentlemen were going to help in whatever was needed, and they would keep in touch with each other. Lucy felt relieved and reassured.

Chapter 41

The Night Before Surgery

The night before her surgery Lucy was anxious, nervous and full of pain. Fibromyalgia pain is known to increase significantly when any organs in the body are injured or stressed. She asked Esteban to come over and spend the night. Previously, he always left after midnight. Lucy was so cold and was shaking so much that she put on flannel pajamas and a cozy thick robe. It was March, and it was quite warm in the house with the heat on. However, Lucy needed that warm comfort from her cuddly night clothes.

Esteban was so happy that she wanted to be with him that night. He was afraid that she may have wanted to be alone. He packed his small overnight bag, and headed over to the big house. He brought some tulips with him to brighten Lucy's mood. He also brought some lavender massage oil to give Lucy a soothing massage. He was very good with his hands.

Lucy went down on the bed almost naked, except for a pair of panties. She put the heat on even higher than it was before. Esteban rubbed her body with strong but very gentle hands. The

123

oil was warmed and provided aroma therapy as well. During the massage Esteban assured Lucy that he would always be there for her – no matter what. She reminded him that she could not bear children. He stroked her face with acceptance and understanding. The atmosphere was silent but powerful. They embraced and kissed for hours. They finally fell asleep in each other's arms.

Chapter 42

In the Hospital and Back Home

Esteban and Claire took off from their regular routines and accompanied Lucy to the hospital. Her complicated surgery was scheduled for Wednesday morning.

The hysterectomy surgery went well as expected. Dr. Adams told them that Lucy's ovaries were quite diseased and pre-cancerous. She definitely could not be a biological mother. When Lucy awakened, Esteban discussed what Doc Adams had said about her surgery and her condition. Lucy cried for five minutes as Esteban embraced her. Lucy could not drink water yet so Esteban fed her ice chips. Claire washed her face and hands with a warm washcloth.

Lucy stayed in the hospital for four days as the doctor believed she needed as much rest and healing as possible. He knew how difficult her life and health had been.

While in the hospital, the roomers did a fantastic job of taking care of things in the house. Agnes took care of Mom, and Martha handled the kitchen. Marty went grocery shopping in his cab. Ezra barbequed steaks one night and did a perfect job of cleaning the grill. All the guys chipped in to pay for the food and helped in the cleanup. The Spanish brothers made enchiladas one night, and Isaac cooked his favorite Chinese delicacies. Claire cooked a Jewish meal of brisket and latkes on Saturday night, and Martha did all the rest. Lucy was flabbergasted with the amount of work and love that the roomers and staff displayed during her hospitalization.

On Sunday morning Marty and Claire brought her home in Marty's taxi. She was so happy to be back home and see everyone, especially Mom. Lucy was still in a great amount of pain and felt much weakness in her muscles. The nurses in the hospital made sure she walked everyday, and gave her strict orders to walk around at home. In the hospital and again at home Lucy received get well cards, flowers, balloons, phone calls and even visits from some of the roomers and friends. However, her biggest surprise was a visit from Esteban's parents in the hospital, and now, they were here for her arrival at home. She did not expect that to happen. They were very warm and cordial and genuinely cared about her. Roberta brought her a beautiful eyelet bed jacket. They even embraced her with hugs and kisses which made her so happy. And, of course Esteban had been with her everyday at the hospital, before and after his work at the university. Lucy had a great deal to look forward to.

After the homecoming everyone ate and conversed, they all went their separate ways except for Esteban, his parents, Mom and Agnes. By the way, Esteban's parents paid for this beautiful homecoming, including dinner and wine. Lucy was still on heavy pain medication, so she had nothing to drink. Esteban told Lucy to open the box, and she did so with great excitement. Inside the box was a lovely and meaningful gold locket. She opened it, and inside was a photo of both of them – smiling happily. Esteban took the photo several weeks before at the fair they both attended. Lucy was so appreciative that she broke out in tears and laughter – at the same time!

Chapter 43

The Conversation

A few days after Lucy came home, Roberta called to see how she was feeling. Lucy felt a bit better every day, but she was still in great distress with pain and weakness. Lucy asked Roberta to please come over, as she wanted to talk with her.

Wednesday evening Roberta came over and brought Lucy some lovely candles. Roberta was such a sport and such a giving individual. Lucy had gotten so fond of her. She was a class act in Lucy's eyes.

Lucy started to tear up and Roberta took her into her arms. Lucy started to babble about not being able to have children. She was so emotional that she started to cry uncontrollably. Roberta sat her down and calmed her with a bottle of water that she always had on her person at all times. Roberta told her that she need not worry about the future. "The future takes care of itself." She told Lucy that she and Esteban could always adopt children. She then told Lucy a little secret that Esteban had just found out. He didn't want to tell Lucy the info as she was so ill with the surgery. Roberta told Lucy that Esteban went to his doctor for a complete physical and blood work. After a few days the doctor called him into his office. He told Esteban that his sperm count was surprisingly low, and that it was unlikely that he could produce a child. Wow, Lucy nearly fell off her chair. They were both unable to have children. They were like two peas in a pod. Lucy felt bad for Esteban but oddly enough, she felt a bit relieved about her own situation. They were even. Roberta told Lucy not to say anything to Esteban, and to allow him to tell her himself. Roberta only told Lucy then because she was so upset.

The two women shared some chamomile tea and Italian biscuits that Lucy always kept in the house. Lucy felt better after the candid conversation and warm treats.

The next day, Esteban came over and took Lucy for a short walk around the property. It was good for Lucy to get out of the house. He then told Lucy about his sexual situation and Lucy just listened as if the info was new to her. She gave Esteban all the moral support and love she had in her heart. They both teared up but held each other together with a close embrace. They both decided that if and when they were married they would plan on adopting children. They had never really talked about marriage before, as there were so many pressing problems going on.

Chapter 44

The Planning

Forty days after Lucy returned home from the hospital, Esteban proposed. She hesitated for a few minutes, but then shouted, a positive "yes." They rejoiced with a hugging session, and then ran upstairs to tell Mom.

By three days later, everyone knew the news, and there was excitement everywhere. It was like someone won the lottery.

Lucy sat down with Esteban and his parents the following evening and the wedding and celebration were discussed. They all decided that having the wedding at Lucy's house and surrounding grounds would be a great location; however, a few days later Lucy was not well, so they all decided it was too much stress for everyone to have it at home. Roberta and Jaime both expressed their wish to pay for most of the wedding. They exclaimed great joy and pride in the future matrimony. They loved Lucy like a daughter and wanted the best for their son. They never saw Esteban so happy and secure in his life.

The wedding was hopefully going to take place September 12th – a Sunday afternoon at El Esplendor Golf and Country Club nearby. The couple wanted the menu to include organic fruits, veggies, and beautiful southwestern dishes. The wedding cake was going to be made by a famous bakery in Phoenix. There was going to be champagne flowing. They all laughed with excitement and happiness. Claire was so thrilled for Lucy. She planned a day out with Lucy to go to Phoenix to look for a wedding gown. Claire had great connections with one exclusive wedding designer. They found a lovely ivory silk and lace gown. It fit Lucy perfectly, as if it was made just for her. Because the owner knew Claire well, the gown was marked down forty percent. Claire paid for a portion of the price and Lucy's mom paid for the rest.

They picked the gown up the following week, as the hem had to be shortened. Lucy was a short pixie-like lady, but she had plenty of curves.

Lucy wanted Mom to be part of the wedding plan, so Lucy couldn't wait to show her the gown. Mom loved the gown, but started to cry. She remembered the last time Lucy tried on a wedding gown, but never had a chance to wear it. Jake had died just weeks before the wedding, and Lucy's life fell apart. Mom was so happy and thrilled that Lucy had another chance.

Invitations were bought at a small paper shop in Nogales, Arizona near Omar's store. They were ivory in color with lace edges – and they resembled Lucy's gown. Lucy found out later that Omar paid for part of the bill.

At times Lucy could not believe that she was again about to be married. Past memories kept on creeping into her mind at times, but she was pretty good at dismissing them and turning them off. She tried to only have positive thoughts in her mind. Enough shattered dreams had happened in her life.

Chapter 45

The Night of the Engagement

Every day was a new day for Lucy. She felt better and better and she and Esteban were becoming inseparable. He slept over every other night and their closeness was enviable.

Lucy started to take better care of herself. She had her hair cut and styled. She got a manicure and a pedicure. And, Esteban took her to every appointment, as she was not supposed to drive, for six to eight weeks. Esteban even took her to a new shiatsu healer that he found at the university where he taught. Lucy felt so much better after her session with Lance, the new healer, that she made two more appointments.

About six weeks after her surgery Esteban took Lucy out to a very special restaurant in Phoenix. He got all dressed up, and he had purchased a beautiful red dress for Lucy to wear. He bought the dress at Claire's department store, and she helped him with the sizing. His favorite color was red. Lucy and Esteban looked like the star couple out on the town, and on the red carpet. They looked outstanding, beautiful, romantically close and statuesque.

After a glass of wine, their main entree and before desert, Esteban took out a little box. Lucy became very excited and anxious, however, she remained very quiet and pensive. Then Esteban peeled off his jacket and lowered to one knee on the floor. Lucy gasped, and Esteban opened the box. He asked Lucy to marry him. The ring was a very sparkly pear-shaped diamond encased in a platinum band. It was just the right size, and it fit Lucy's finger perfectly. The two lovers kissed and hugged. Everyone in that very exclusive restaurant got up and cheered. This was a very special evening! It was spectacular!

Chapter 46

The Engagement Party

Two weeks later Roberta and Jaime gave the two lovers a beautiful engagement party. It also took place at El Esplendor, the large hotel and golf resort in Rio Rico. It was a beautiful day in May, but the temperature rose to over one hundred and four degrees.

The party was held on a Sunday at 4:00PM. The guests included all the roomers and their partners. It included all the help and their loved ones. Esteban's favorite students and fellow professors and their "besties" attended, and Esteban's parents' friends also attended. It was a congenial crowd, and the main theme was love and joy.

About 6:30PM everyone who brought their bathing suit changed inside and then jumped in the pool. Oh what fun it was.

Lucy wore a pale mint green dress that evening and later jumped into a sexy black bathing suit. Esteban wore a white silk shirt and white silk trousers. He later wore a navy blue knit swim suit cut very short in the legs. Wow,

Esteban was feeling mighty sexy and confident those days.

The couple received lots of presents and even cash. And, Roberta and Jaime paid for the entire party.

Chapter 47

David Came Back

Six days before the wedding day, there was a loud knock on the front door. Lucy looked out the window panes of the door and became shocked. David, her long-lost roomer and lover was back in town. He left Arizona, went back to his wife to try working on the marriage again, and there he stood as handsome as ever. Lucy opened the door, and David rushed in to hug her with great fervor.

Lucy was completely confused with her emotions. Suddenly she remembered how much she cared for this man, but then guilty feelings took over in her mind. She was going to be married to Esteban. She truly loved Esteban, and this sudden surprise of seeing David was absolutely blowing her mind.

He came in and sat down in the living room / dining room like he had never left. His smiles were gracious and real, but Lucy noticed a great sadness in his eyes. He told Lucy that his marriage was definitely over. His wife ran away with the children, and she met a gentleman from their country club. He was much older than her –

but very wealthy. David finally found out where his children lived, but they were quite far away – states away.

David had gotten his old job back at Davis-Monthan, and he had hoped he could renew his love affair with Lucy. However, Lucy very quickly notified David that she was to be married the next week. She told him she loved her Esteban, and nothing or no person could stand in her way. She told David she would always treasure their moments together, and always care about him.

They hugged for a good five minutes, and then Lucy started to cry. She truly cared about David. He was a very good man. But, their love affair was definitely over. David told Lucy that he would always stay in touch with her, and, if she ever needed anything he would be there for her.

Chapter 48

Wedding Planning

Lucy and Esteban made an appointment with the wedding staff at El Esplendor. The wedding planners were Sandra and Adriana. They were both so helpful and enthusiastic. Adriana was due to have her baby in two weeks. Wow. She was huffing and puffing as she took them down to the main ballroom. The ballroom was huge, so everyone decided that half of the ballroom would be adequate for the one hundred and twenty-five to one hundred and thirty guests that probably would attend.

The couple imagined how beautiful the room would look with the round tables all decorated with lavender and beige tablecloths and accessories. The room's crystal chandeliers were massive and elegant. The room would be perfect. Sandra gave them all the information and the prices of each package. Lucy and Esteban had to take care of the purchase of the flowers and accessories, but Roberta and Jaime later took care of that. They also had to find the right rabbi to perform their marriage ceremony. They later found an amazing reform rabbi in Tucson who advised them on the correct rituals of a Jewish wedding. He would definitely come to Rio Rico to perform the sacred ceremony. Lucy told Rabbi she wanted to convert to Judaism at some time in the future, and he told her she would make a wonderful Jewess.

Sandra was extremely helpful in explaining everything including all the available choices. Lucy and Esteban picked the best wedding package as they wanted the perfect wedding of their dreams.

Chapter 49

Wedding Invites

The wedding which was to take place on Sunday, May 12th at 4:00PM. Invitations were mailed out twenty-one days before the wedding date. One hundred and twenty-five invites were sent and one hundred positive replies came back.

Esteban's parents had business associates, family members from all over the world, and a close network of friends who were all invited. Esteban invited fellow professors and teachers at the University of Arizona, and of course his immediate group of good friends.

Lucy only had a handful of family and even fewer friends. Her family and friends were really the gentlemen roomers and everyone who worked around the house. All the roomers and their partners, best friends and immediate family were invited, and, they were all thrilled and excited to come.

Chapter 50

Wedding Attire

The colors of the wedding were champagne and shades of purple.

Mom's dress was lilac (pink tone) color and was embossed with tiny pearls and rosebuds. The rosebuds were a bit darker than the dress. The jacket of the dress was lilac cashmere with the tiny pearls and rosebuds around the collar. She wore matching silk shoes, small champagne pearl earrings and her old and priceless diamond rings. Her dress was sleeveless and mid-length. She looked healthy and beautiful. She was amazing.

Claire's dress was a deep lavender (blue tone) color taffeta maxi dress – long sleeve with small diamond-like stones around the low cut neckline. Her shoes matched exactly. Her jewelry consisted of a diamond bracelet, a very large amethyst ring and small diamond studs in her ears. She also wore a dainty amethyst choker around her neck.

Agnes wore a medium-shaded purple knit dress and jacket. The outfit was floor length and had braiding around the collar and cuffs. She loved crystal jewelry and wore matching earrings, bracelet and a giant crystal broach!

Roberta wanted to dress like a Spanish matron. She wore a lavender silk blouse with deep purple ruffles down the center, with a champagne silk tuxedo suit. Her hair was tied back in a chignon wrapped around with champagne pearls and lavender crystals. How gorgeous and regal.

Jaime, Esteban and Andy wore champagne color tuxedos with matching shirts and shoes. Their bow ties and cummerbunds were deep purple. Andy was Esteban's best man. The three men looked exceptionally handsome and classy.

Lucy's gown was exquisite and feminine. It was pale lavender silk with champagne lace and baby pearls embossed all over the floor length gown. It had short puffy sleeves. Her hair was curled even more than usual, and she wore it back with baby champagne pearls around the top and back. Her shoes matched the lace of the gown. Her jewelry consisted of an amethyst heart necklace, diamond earrings and bracelet, and her diamond engagement and wedding rings. Her rings were handed down from Roberta's mother who loved large diamonds. She died some eighteen years ago.

The rest of the gentlemen roomers wore dark suits, lavender or lilac shirts and dark ties and shoes.

Chapter 51

The Wedding and Honeymoon

The wedding took place as planned and everything went smoothly. Almost everyone invited attended, and the gifts were amazing and so useful. The couple also collected some monies and Esteban's parents gave them five-thousand dollars besides paying for the flowers, the rabbi, and all the decorations and accessories. Wow! Lucy, Mom, Claire and Roberta all had matching small bouquets of magnificent violets and pansies in several shades of purple.

Claire's brother was a photographer and he volunteered to take photos and a video for very little money. His wife was also invited to the wedding.

Everyone danced for hours to a three piece band that happened to be friends of Andy. They all went to school together, and two of them even worked with Andy at the plant.

The hotel banquet hall looked elegant and excitingly festive. All night, guests were raving about the entire wedding ceremony.

Before the wedding, Lucy and Esteban joined a reform synagogue in Tucson. The couple,

151

especially Lucy, wanted to learn about Jewish culture – the customs and traditions. They also desired to know all about the religions aspects of the Jewish wedding ceremony. The rabbi, Thomas Louchheim met with them several times to discuss the wedding ceremony, to discuss their dreams and wishes, and to inform them about future Jewish life. He also met with them for a three hour class in Judaic studies. He was thorough, understanding, and very kind.

Lucy also informed Rabbi that she wanted to convert to Judaism in the near future.

Lucy wanted Jaime to walk her down the isle, as they both felt like father and daughter. He was delighted that she asked him. He was so proud of her as a strong, kind and intelligent woman.

The ceremony was beautiful and very emotional. Rabbi spoke about the great love of Esteban and Lucy compared to the great love of Abraham and Sarah in the Old Testament. When the ceremony ended and Esteban smashed the glass with his hard shoe, the couple embraced and kissed for a good five minutes.

The couple honeymooned in Spain and Turkey, as Esteban wanted to look up some older relatives of his parents who still remained there.

Roberta and Jaime helped Esteban pay for the honeymoon. What a generous couple and, don't forget they only had one child. The honeymoon proved to be a wonderfully exciting time for Lucy and Esteban. They relaxed some, met some wonderful relatives, and visited some special historic sites. They never spent more than two hours away from each other. They enjoyed being with each other so much.

When the couple honeymooned, everyone looked after Mom. Agnes stayed five full days and overnight too. Roberta and Jaime stayed with her several hours on the weekends, and the gentlemen roomers helped out also. The part-time housekeeper prepared meals and did some of the laundry.

When the newlyweds returned home, the house was clean and everything was in order. The three pussycats missed Lucy so much that they hung onto her clothes and shoes. They ran circles around her and would not leave her alone.

When things settled down Esteban and Lucy were on their way to a happy life together. Esteban moved in with Lucy and everyone accepted him as family.

Chapter 52

Lucy and Esteban Six Months Later

Lucy and Esteban were inseparable and their love was impenetrable. No one could come between them at that time. Esteban completed his doctorate degree and obtained full professorship.

Around five to six months after the couple's wondrous marriage, Esteban found out about a terrible and tragic accident. One of Esteban's fellow professors and his lovely wife, whom Esteban knew pretty well, had been killed in a major car and truck crash. There were no survivors. Esteban was completely saddened and shocked by the news. He also found out that they left a little daughter. Her name was Irisa, and she was beautiful and now alone. Her parents were from Hungary, and she spoke some English and some Hungarian. Lucy asked Esteban if she could stay with them for awhile. After all, Irisa was only five years old, and Lucy would love a little girl in the house. After three months the newlyweds were totally in love with this child. They wanted to keep her as their own. She had no other real family, and they could provide her with a good life and lots of love. The proper paper work was filed, and the new parents were overjoyed with welcoming this precious little girl into their family. All the roomers and friends also fell in love with this redheaded, blue-eyed munchkin.

Even with a child, Lucy and Esteban always made time to make love at least four or five times a week. They desired each other more and more as time passed.

Lucy also celebrated more and more of Jewish customs and traditions. She learned from Jaime and Roberta, and she also read Jewish history books that she bought, or rented from the library there.

Regarding her health, Lucy's fibromyalgia condition remained just about the same. Through the months, Lucy had her good days – and her bad ones. Many days she still had to rest in bed, especially after Irisa came into their lives. She took some new supplements like magnesium malic acid which seemed to really help the stiffness and pain. She also found a wonderful new shiatsu healer and attended his sessions once every week. The sessions really helped with stress also.

Chapter 53

Roberta and Jaime
Six Months Later

Roberta and Jaime remained even closer to Lucy and Esteban. They were very generous with their time and money. They got very close to Mom and spent one or two evenings a week with Lucy, Esteban, and Mom too.

They fell in love with Irisa and spoiled her to pieces. They took her to the movies, for walks, and to the playground too.

Jaime had some back surgery but the results were very good and positive. He only had to take off from work for four weeks. Jaime worked some days in their accounting office, and Roberta worked other days. Only around tax time did they both work in the practice.

At one time after having supper at Jaime and Roberta's home, did the in-laws admit a secret to Lucy and Esteban. Even Esteban did not know this secret. Esteban was in shock listening to his father speak. He thought he knew everything about his parents. However, he did not. Jaime told the couple that he and his wife were also in the CIA as well as being certified accountants. While one worked in the office, the other one traveled not too far away on assignment. They both spoke four languages and also loved being agents or assets. When Esteban was very young Roberta took him with her to the office, and as he got older, he always had a part-time nanny. Esteban and Lucy were in shock, especially Esteban! He could not fully comprehend the news. However, as time went by the young couple accepted everything.

Chapter 54

The Cats
Six Months Later

Callie lost a little weight and Yoda gained some. Yoda would follow Lucy around begging for food. He was becoming a nuisance – but a charming one.

Callie wanted to sleep with Lucy and Esteban more and more, and they had to make room for her in the bed. She didn't want to sleep at the bottom of the bed; she wanted to sleep on a pillow between the couple. She was a real lady cat.

There was a definite problem with Lando. He was almost sixteen years old and he had just developed diabetes. He had to get insulin shots twice a day. He also had lost almost four pounds, which is a lot for a cat. Esteban changed his litter box almost twice a day, as with diabetes, cats urinate very often. Lando was a real trooper – he tried very hard at everything. His hair was severely matted now and Lucy tried to brush and comb out the knots every day. Lando was a

159

sweet and very grateful cat. He licked everyone and purred all the time.

Chapter 55

Agnes
Six Months Later

Agnes went to Weight Watchers for almost two months and lost over twenty-three pounds. She looked so much better and she felt so much better. She continued to lose weight slowly and went to almost every weekly meeting.

Agnes's former boyfriend, now husband Bryan suffered a heart attack and she had to stay at home more often. She only came to take care of Mom three to five hours a day, and only four days a week. She still always remained a faithful employee and friend of the family – and especially Mom. Lucy and Esteban contributed money toward Agnes's husband's medical bills.

·

Chapter 56

Andy
Six Months Later

Andy was now twenty-four years old, and, he was still the youngest roomer in the house. He still looked like a young boy with a constant blush on his face and bright pink lips. You still wanted to give him a tight hug, as his dark eyes still portrayed emotional hurts from years ago.

Andy received his Bachelors of Science degree, and was taking classes for his Masters of Business Administration degree. The company that he worked for was willing to totally pay for all his future school expenses if he remained working at the manufacturing plant. They even promised him a good-size raise along with more responsibility.

Andy became even closer to Annette, his half-sister. Annette's aunt with whom she had lived, suddenly died from a heart attack. It was quite a shock to both Annette and Andy. Annette's aunt had left their small house to Annette. It was a two bedroom, one big bath house on a quiet street. The brother and sister talked about Andy moving in with Annette. He

163

thought it was a great idea. They figured it would happen in the next few months.

Chapter 57

Marty
Six Months Later

Marty felt much older and slightly confused about his life. He still loved driving his cab, but he felt like he needed more diversions. He needed to feel more important. His health was still good, and he did work out two to three days a week. He was still involved with Claire, and their love grew even stronger. He was still not making a lot of money, and whatever he did make, he gave a great deal to his grandchildren. He still saw his family and grandchildren at least once a week.

Claire had a great idea for Marty. She felt since he loved children and he was somewhat great at sports, that perhaps he could coach the local baseball team for teens. He thought about it for a few weeks and finally agreed. He really became excited to do something different. He later became quite good working with the kids, and they adored his personality and strength of character.

Chapter 58

Claire
Six Months Later

Claire and Marty were a great pair. They really enjoyed each other's company and saw each other almost every day. They even spoke about moving in together at Claire's place. Marty was considering it.

Claire had received a good promotion in her job and the owner, who was retiring, made her an offer of co-ownership of the department store. She was both thrilled and humbled. However, Claire was quite confident that she could do a very good job.

Claire's rheumatoid arthritis was still severe, but she began taking a new experimental drug that was helping somewhat. It also had a few side effects such as insomnia, and Claire definitely needed her sleep. The good thing about her new co-ownership was that she could take a little more time off – if needed.

Claire and Lucy remained as close as ever and Claire loved Irisa.

The Gentlemen's Rooming House

Chapter 59

Omar
Six Months Later

Omar continued to work very hard at the store since he now was paying off his ownership of the business. The business was slowly building up and the customers always seemed to adore Omar. He believed the customers had to be happy with their purchases.

One day a young woman came into the store and was shopping when Omar noticed her. His eyes did not leave her face. She was exquisite. Her long blond hair was new for Omar and, her blue eyes reminded him of the ocean that he hadn't seen for a very long time.

He started to speak with her, and before they knew it the store was ready to close.

Omar asked her out for some supper and she agreed. They went out to a little Spanish restaurant and conversed for over two hours after they actually ate. Her name was Ava and she was visiting from Ohio. She was a high school teacher in Spanish, of all things, and she loved Mexico and Arizona immensely. Later

Omar told Ava his life story and he learned by surprise that Ava was also Jewish. What a match. Hopefully, things would continue after Ava went home.

Chapter 60

Isaac
Six Months Later

Isaac was doing very well. He was working out some, and he was doing more and more martial arts. He and Leon were practicing tai chi also. Isaac and his lady friend Kara got much closer, and they were almost inseparable when they each had time off. Isaac loved cooking with Kara, as she was a fine cook also. In fact, they both gained ten pounds, and they both looked much better.

Isaac was offered a new and better position in the restaurant where he worked for seven years. He became executive chef and assistant manager. He received a good raise, and, the owner picked him up every morning and drove him home every evening. That way, Isaac wouldn't have to ride by bike. He wore more light colored clothes, and even white once in a while. Remember, years before he only wore black or dark brown. Isaac was so much more happy with his life.

The Gentlemen's Rooming House

Chapter 61

Ezra
Six Months Later

Ezra lost some thirty pounds with Weight Watchers just like Agnes. They went to meetings together once in a while.

Ezra and Leon were still close and loving, and Ezra gave Leon more responsibility.

Ezra became even more religious, and he recited Bible quotes all the time. Sometimes it was a bit annoying, but you could not ever not love Ezra. He still remained a bus driver, and had received a good raise. He was able to purchase a good little used car, so now he was able to drive Leon and himself to church on Sundays, and on other occasions. That was a real problem before. Ezra still was very helpful to Lucy and her mom.

Chapter 62

Leon
Six Months to One Year Later

Since Ezra lost weight, so did Leon. He also walked a lot with his dad. They started an exercise and diet regimen.

Leon received a promotion at the supermarket where he worked. He was learning to become a part-time cashier, but he knew that it may take years to train him. However, he was excited about the project.

Leon received a good-size raise during his training, and he used the money for the movies and pizza night. He was proud of being able to pay for more things.

He also made two new friends who just moved near the supermarket. They were two girls, and they always treated Leon with respect.

Isaac and Leon still practiced different karate moves every week, and Leon became more and more confident and strong everyday.

Leon even met another young lady who had similar problems like himself. Her name was

175

Laura and they started to do things together. Laura lived at home with her parents, but she was able to see Leon at least two to three times a week. There was always one parent present when the two were together.

Ezra was so proud of his son, and they remained as close as ever.

Chapter 63

Paul and Joe
Six Months to One Year Later

Both men did well at work and with their children. Joe's son started college and worked two jobs to help his dad pay for tuition. Paul's daughter finished college and was pregnant with her first child – Paul's first grandchild.

The brothers still worked very hard and were saving their money.

Paul was still with Margo and they were married at the big house four months after Lucy's wedding. Lucy paid for a beautiful and somewhat lavish wedding for the new couple. They had all their sixteen cousins and their families come to their wedding. They were such a magnificent couple. Margo, with her stupendously long black shiny hair and bright blue eyes. And, Paul with his new cool-cut haircut, his tight-fitting white tuxedo, and his bright plaid vest.

After the wedding, Paul moved into Margo's home, and Eric, the brothers' cousin moved in with Joe. Everyone was happy.

Chapter 64

James and Roger Six Months Later

James became more aware of his clothes and how he dressed, and he toned down his style somewhat. He even started to eat chicken, fish and turkey. However, he only ate when he was starving. He still believed Americans were gluttonous and greedy creatures.

He still was substitute teaching – but only for high school, and he was tutoring more and more. He tutored more than ten students at one time during any given week. He still absolutely adored Roger, and their relationship remained as strong as ever. Computer life, tutoring, working out and loving Roger was James' whole life.

Roger lost some twenty-five pounds and he felt great. He still was managing the large warehouse, and it was almost his sixteenth year doing so. He still loved James as much as ever, and was involved with his son Nathan at least twice a week. He and Nate were speaking about life more now, and Roger tried to explain his gay life and his decision to follow his heart and mind.

179

Nathan was very interested, and tried to understand his father much more now. Nathan also was dating a young lady now, and he wanted his dad to meet her.

Chapter 65

Lucy and Esteban
One Year Later

Esteban became a full-time professor at the University of Arizona, and he loved his students. He taught English literature, philosophy and the humanities. His classes were always filled with devoted students. He also spent some time doing recruiting for new CIA agents at the university. He loved doing that also; but he had to be very careful not to overlap the two positions.

Lucy became very engrossed in her motherly duties and, in taking care of her health. Her fibromyalgia at times became so bad that she had to stay in bed for days at a time. She was very close to Esteban's parents and they were so grateful to have her and Irisa in their lives. They were also good to Mom.

Lucy was still studying Hebrew, Jewish customs and the traditions with Rabbi Louchheim. She was becoming a devoted Jewess.

About nine months after their marriage Lucy and Esteban found out about a little one year old boy from Vietnam. His mother died at childbirth, and his father was nowhere to be found. He somehow was taken from a shelter in Vietnam to a private adoption agency in Phoenix. Esteban heard about this adorable little boy from a colleague who was a friend and a lawyer. He told Esteban that dozens of children were taken from this particular shelter and transported to America by a private couple from Phoenix who had visited Vietnam months before. They were saddened by how bad the living conditions were for the children. They worked endlessly and spent thousands of dollars to bring the children to America. Finally, almost a year after they started the project, dozens of other young children were transported to the adoption agency in Phoenix. The couple were older but they never had children, so they even adopted two of the children. When Esteban's friend told him about the children, Esteban and Lucy went to the agency to see them. Lucy was very excited to possibly find a sibling for Irisa. As it was, they found one little Vietnamese boy to be their choice. Immediately when Lucy saw that adorable little face, they knew that they wanted this child to be in their family.

Lucy and Esteban took the child home with them. He had very black curly hair, tan smooth skin like silk, and big dark eyes like black saucers. They named him Ralph after Esteban's lawyer friend who found out about the agency and the boy. When they took him home everyone at the big house absolutely fell in love with him. Irisa took him in her arms and hugged him tightly. She said, "have a new brother toy", and everyone laughed.

Lucy and Esteban were immensely grateful for their two wonderful children, and became fantastic parents to them. Everyone in the big house admired them and also took part somewhat in the lives of the children.

Irisa loved Ralph and helped take care of him like a little mother.

The Gentlemen's Rooming House

Chapter 66

Roberta and Jaime One Year Later

Roberta and Jaime remained as close as ever, to each other and to their children. They considered Lucy, Irisa and now little Ralph all their children, besides Esteban of course.

They spent less time in the field as CIA assets, as they wanted to spend as much time as possible with the family.

Chapter 67

Mom
Her Last Fifteen Months

After the wedding, Mom became more and more ill. Her cancer had spread to her lungs, and she had a very hard time breathing. She was in the hospital and The Lung & Sleep Institute several times. She lived to see both Irisa and Ralph, and the joy that the children brought to Lucy and Esteban, and everyone around the big house.

She died fifteen months after Lucy's wedding. Over forty people attended her funeral, and she definitely was a woman that everyone would miss for years to come. Lucy missed her immensely.

The Gentlemen's Rooming House

Chapter 68

The Cats
One Year Later

After the wedding, Lando the cat became more and more ill due to his diabetes. Lucy took him to different veterinarians and animal hospitals for the best treatments and he did remain status quo for quite a long time. However, one day in March he just couldn't breathe and he lost all his normal faculties. They took him to the emergency vet and they had to put Lando to sleep.

Everyone cried that day and the next and the next. The other two cats Callie and Yoda grieved in their own way. They looked all over the big house for Lando and both cats slept with Lucy and Esteban with Lando's collar. The cats' eyes watered for days.

Little by little things got back to normal, but there was always a void in the pantry where Lando had slept. Lucy had Lando for sixteen years and she missed him a great deal.

It took months until Yoda became more fun-loving and happy. The cats seemed to look lonely and needed a great deal of affection. Callie and Yoda even became better friends – after all they only had each other plus the grownups of course.

Chapter 69

Marty and Claire One Year Later

Marty finally moved into Claire's home, and they were married six weeks later. Lucy gave Claire a wedding shower and the big event was also held at the big house. The wedding reception was beautiful and a justice of the peace married the pair. Claire's one cousin and Marty's children and grandchildren all attended.

Chapter 70

Omar
One Year Later

Omar and Ava had been conversing for over six months now and Omar talked Ava into moving to Arizona. She could always get a job teaching in Arizona, and they really wanted to live together. Ava agreed and she made plans after the school year to move. They would later find a big enough apartment for the two of them to hopefully share their love and a new future together.

Chapter 71

Isaac
One Year Later

Isaac was still doing very well. His new and better position in the restaurant lifted his ego and his self-esteem. And, Isaac learned to drive a car, and he even bought a used little Honda. Now his big boss didn't have to pick him up to go to work. Isaac and Kara became very close and even talked about sharing an apartment together.

Chapter 72

Agnes
One Year Later

Agnes met another gentleman friend at the supermarket, and he moved in with her. They both worked part time and her home was paid for, so they started to just really enjoy their free time together. Neither one wanted or needed to marry. Thank G-d.

Chapter 73

Andy
One Year Later

Andy moved in with his half-sister Annette, and everything was good. He still remained close to Esteban and Lucy, and Annette became close to them also. They were invited to the big house often. Andy was still doing well at school and at work.

Chapter 74

James and Roger
One Year Later

Things were pretty much the same with the guys except both men befriended a new much younger man who was a friend of Roger's son Nathan. His name was Zack and he lived alone. Nathan was with a young lady now, so James and Roger became very close to Zack. He had no family, and the guys even suggested that Zack rent a unit at the big house. They loved Zack's sense of humor and his gentleness. They wanted to do things together. Zack was not gay.

Chapter 75

Ezra
One Year Later

Ezra lost even more weight walking with Leon before work. Leon even lost some eighteen pounds also, and he felt great.

Ezra met a very nice lady at church who lost her husband some years back. She was a little younger than Ezra but they seemed to have a lot in common. She never had any children and she shared a lot of time with Leon also.

She was very religious like Ezra and they went to Bible study three times a week besides Sunday service.

In Memoriam: Lando the Cat

11/01/1998 – 03/05/2015